"WHY RESEARCH ME?" MONTGOMERIE DEMANDED

Xorialle spread his hands appealingly. "Nothing personal, my boy. My survey turned up a number of possibilities as test subjects. I selected you."

"What kind of test?"

"Oh, a standard wide-band evaluation—in your case with the emphasis on potential, of course. There would be no point in attempting one based on your present physical and mental condition. We already have your unfortunate culture as ample evidence of your kind's ineptitude at this stage in solving even the most elementary societal problems."

"What do you mean by 'my kind'?" Dammy said suspiciously. "Is that some kind of crack?"

"Your kind, my dear lad: your race, tribe, breed, species, call it what you will."

"You talk," Dammy said carefully, eyeing Xorialle gingerly, "as if you weren't included."

KEITH LAUMER
THE
ULTIMAX
MAN

BAEN
BOOKS

THE ULTIMAX MAN

This is a work of fiction. All the characters and events portrayed in this book are fictional, and any resemblance to real people or incidents is purely coincidental.

A Baen Book

Baen Publishing Enterprises
260 Fifth Avenue
New York, N.Y. 10001

First Baen printing, June 1987

ISBN: 0-671-65652-X

Cover art by J.K. Potter

Printed in the United States of America

Distributed by
SIMON & SCHUSTER
1230 Avenue of the Americas
New York, N.Y. 10020

One

A man walked slowly along a darkened street. He was a young man, conservatively attired in a dark blue double-breasted blazer, gray bell-bottoms, and a bright blue shirt with a wide regimental tie. But he moved like a man of eighty, holding his elbow pressed tightly to his side. His name was Damocles Montgomerie and he had been shot at close range by a .32 caliber Beretta automatic pistol, the bullet having broken two ribs and driven a dozen bone splinters into his liver before coming to rest half an inch from his spine.

Reaching an alley mouth, he half-turned, half-fell into the shadowy space between corroded brick walls. A garbage can lid clattered on oily cobbles. He braced himself against the wall, pushed himself upright, and went on, deeper into the reek of garbage. Reaching the end of the cul-de-sac, he turned, put his back to the wall. With his fingers, he explored the hot, damp area below the ribs on the right side. There was a neat hole in the thick flannel of the coat, a hole that continued on through the heavy silk shirt and the fitted undershirt into the flesh beneath.

A step sounded softly from the direction of the alley mouth. The beam of a flashlight speared out, traversed the pavement, played up the wall and across Montgomerie's chest, moved to his face. It held there for a moment and then winked out.

"Where you want it, punk?" a soft, hoarse voice rasped. "Between the eyes suit you OK?"

"Better try a gut shot, Chico," Montgomerie said in a voice as thin and taut as a stretched wire. "I don't trust your aim."

"Save it, rat. You got five seconds to square it with the man upstairs. One . . ."

He listened to the count. It seemed to go on and on. Then it reached five. Light blossomed from the muzzle of the gun, illuminating the scene with a warm yellow glow. The plume of flame elongated, ringed with viscid smoke which slowed, stiffened into immobility. The killer stood, feet apart, leaning forward, his left arm out, fingers spread, the gun in his right fist thrust out before him. His lips were pulled back from his teeth; his eyes were half-closed, intent, unmoving. . . .

Behind him, something stirred near the alley mouth. A slightly built man in a gray derby and a dapper morning coat complete with ascot and boutonniere was picking his way fastidiously back toward the little tableau so curiously arrested. His face—visible by its own pale glow—was narrow, elderly, prim, with a neatly groomed hairline mustache. He swung a slim silver-headed cane from one pigskin-gloved hand, glanced curiously at the immobile gunner as he edged past him, came to a halt before the injured man. He looked him over assessingly, his lips pursed in an expression of mild disapproval.

You seem to have managed your affairs very badly, my lad, a perfectly clear voice spoke inside Montgomerie's head.

He tried to speak; nothing happened. He tried to move: same result.

Tush, no need to grow excited. Nothing will happen to you that hasn't happened to uncounted billions of other organisms in the short history of the planet.

HELP, Montgomerie yelled silently. *GET ME OUT OF HERE.*

Exactly my intention, my boy. Simply be calm. In fact . . . it might be as well if you'd just drop off to sleep . . .

A heavy curtain of drowsiness wrapped itself around Montgomerie's thoughts. He was dimly aware of the old gentleman stepping briskly closer, clamping him under an arm, and walking up into the air. He caught one fading glimpse of tarred rooftops, ventilators, TV antennae, dropping away below. Then he let it all go and slid, faster and faster, down into the bottomless vortex of unconsciousness.

This, Damocles reflected contentedly, *is what I call living. Snoozing away in a first-class seat on a luxury airliner bound for the hot spots of gay Paree. Out the window, the moon will be shining down on the billows, and in a second or two the stewardess will ease up to me and say . . .*

"Care for a sandwich, lad?" said a ratchety male voice. Montgomerie's eyes flew open. He was in a tiny room, seated in a semireclining chair before a curved surface of black glass. Below the glass was a cluster of bright-colored knobs. On one of the knobs rested a thin, veined hand. The hand was attached to a crisp white French cuff which emerged from a well-pressed black sleeve which led inevitably up along an arm to a gently smiling, wizened face with thin white hair and a fingernail mustache.

"You!" Dammy piped in a voice like a baby bird. "But . . ."

"You were perhaps hoping to see Chico?"

"Chico!" Dammy winced, and felt a pang in his side. He fingered the site of the bullet wound and felt smooth, thick padding. "I thought—how—what—"

"Don't trouble yourself, Damocles. I've sealed the puncture and given you a temporary metabolic hold to prevent further deterioration in your condition until I can whisk you into the automed. In the meantime, a bite to eat will no doubt reinforce your sense of security."

"What sense of security?" Montgomerie chirped, and paused to rest. "I thought I dreamed you. While I was dying, I mean."

"Ummnn, not precisely. You perceived me with a portion of your cerebrum not usually activated in the waking state—but this is a side effect of the stasis field, no doubt."

"You're not—the Angel Gabriel or anybody like that?"

"Another branch of the service entirely. Would you prefer pastrami, corned beef, or Swiss cheese?"

"Wait a minute," Dammy expostulated. "Just hold on a minute. Who are you? Where am I? How did I get here? And—"

"You may call me Xorialle. You're aboard my cycler. I brought you here."

" 'Sorry Al.' That's not much of a name. I'll just

call you Al, OK?" Dammy closed his eyes tightly. "I got shot. That's definite, Al. It hurts." He gave his side a prod to reassure himself. "After that, I was in an alley . . . and Chico . . ." He paused to swallow. "Funny, I never figured you'd have time to see the flash from the slug that blew your brains out. But . . ." He fingered his head. "At that range, how could he miss?"

"He didn't," Xorialle said. "That is to say, the bullet was projected along a path intersecting the point in space occupied a moment before by your left eye and continuing, doubtless, to impact against the wall."

Dammy's hand went involuntarily to his eye. It seemed intact.

"Uh-uh," he said. "I don't believe in that life after death theory, Al."

"Of course," Xorialle continued, "by the time the bullet left the gun, you were no longer there."

"I . . . ducked?"

"Not at all, my dear fellow. I removed you from the line of fire. If it weren't for my intervention, your existence as a conscious intellect would have been terminated twelve minutes ago."

"Yeah, but how could you? I mean, I saw you coming. And after that . . . I was floating in the air; and the gun . . ."

"I suppose you're referring to the other side-effects of the stasis field. It was necessary, you know. I don't have the facilities for reconstructing cerebra; I need you intact."

"Hold it right there," Dammy cut in. "If this is your idea of a job offer, forget it. I work alone. If you had something to do with . . . what happened back there, OK, thanks. I don't get it, but that's OK too. So I'll just be on my way now, and . . ."

"And be dead in six hours," Xorialle said casually. "Your liver, you know. Can't function very well with a quarter-ounce of bone chips in it. Quite inoperable by local techniques, of course. Your only hope is my automed."

"You a doctor?" Dammy inquired weakly.

"You may be assured your case is well within my competence."

"How do I know you're not lying?"

"Ummnn. I've been suppressing the symptoms of your injury. Possibly that's given you a false sense of well-being . . ."

Someone lit a match in Dammy's gizzard. It flared up, ignited a large wad of excelsior someone had left lying in the vicinity. He opened his mouth to yell, and the fire winked out and was gone as if it had never been.

"That's how you'd feel if I weren't, er, handling your case," Xorialle said crisply. "Shall I continue?"

"I was going to ask you how you did that," Dammy gasped, "but never mind. I wouldn't understand the answer. Let's get going to the hospital."

"ETA approximately forty-five minutes," the oldster said briskly.

"How do you get out of here?" Dammy was groping at the strap holding him to his chair.

"I wouldn't suggest releasing the harness," Xorialle said casually. "We're at five hundred thousand feet, traveling at approximately Mach 7."

Montgomerie clutched for support. "I don't believe a word of it," he said, and swallowed hard. "We're standing still. I'm scared of airplanes. That is, I would be if I'd ever been in one. There's nothing holding them up. And I don't know much about it, maybe, but I know they make plenty of racket, and—"

"At one hundred miles altitude there's no air to speak of, hence no turbulence, no rush of wind. And since the cycler's engines are silent, quite naturally you hear nothing."

"Where's my p-parachute?" Dammy inquired in a voice that had a distressing tendency to slip into a falsetto.

"My boy, if you should, through some malfunction of the safety interlocks, manage to eject yourself from the cycler, you'd be shredded into ribbons and toasted to a crisp before you fell halfway to the surface. I'm afraid a parachute wouldn't help."

"That makes me feel a lot better," Dammy said in a tightly controlled voice. "If it wasn't for a couple things like Chico's gun and that little trick you did with my insides a minute ago, I'd call your bluff."

"No bluff, my lad. Simply accept the fact that your life has been fortuitously extended, and conduct yourself accordingly."

"Where are we going? We must be halfway to the North Pole by now."

ETA 42 minutes and 12.4 seconds, to be precise," Xorialle said. "You'll see it shortly. In the meantime—what about a Bavarian ham on rye and a cold glass of Pilsner?"

The rock thrust up out of the Arctic Sea—a hundred-yard-high boulder all alone in the vast whitecapped sweep of frigid ink-black ocean, crowned by a cluster of lights that sprang into being in response to a button poked by Xorialle as he maneuvered the cycler down from the heights.

"Kind of isolated, isn't it?" Montgomerie inquired rhetorically, noting the slow wash of breakers at the base of the outcropping.

"My work requires a certain exclusiveness," Xorialle explained offhandedly. "Far better to choose a spot where one is unlikely to be disturbed than to be put to the bother of disposing of intruders, which frequently leads to more trespassers in search of the original ones and more disposals."

Dammy gave Xorialle a searching look.

"Disposals, huh?"

"Quite humanely, of course—to employ the word in its theoretical sense." Xorialle gave Montgomerie a friendly smile. "No offense intended to your race, of course."

"What's my race got to do with it? I'm as blue-eyed and sandy-haired as the next guy."

"Everything, my boy, everything. But I'll make all that clear to you very soon, after I've attended to repairing your hurts."

The craft settled smoothly toward a circular opening that irised wide to receive them. Walls rose around them; the cycler touched with a faint jar and was still. Xorialle touched a button and the hatch popped open. Dammy, braced for an icy blast, felt only the soft caress of a tropical night laden with the aroma of frangipani and magnolias and a faint melody of Hawaiian guitars. He stepped down, favoring his punctured side, gazed around mutely at the flower beds, pool, terraces, and palms. Above him spread what appeared to be an ordinary Tahitian night sky.

"Do you find the environment congenial?" Xorialle said with a note of concern.

"If you mean do I like the layout, yeah, it's OK."

"Splendid; now we'd best hurry along to the laboratory. That metabolic hold won't keep you alive forever."

Dammy started to ask a question, but at that moment his words were cut off by a twinge probably resembling the sensation experienced by a vampire when impaled by a stake. He suppressed a groan and followed the old man across the patio through a wide, doorless arch and along a green-tiled passage to a walnut slab door which opened on a chamber asparkle with white enamel and polished chrome.

"You find the decorative scheme reassuring, I trust?" Xorialle said with a note of pride. "I assure you no effort has been spared to reproduce an authentic setting, complete with full sensory stimuli."

"At least it doesn't smell like a hospital," Dammy commented.

"Eh? Oh, to be sure." Xorialle turned and touched a button. The acrid reek of ether, carbolic acid, poached eggs, and deodorant sprang instantly into being.

"Soothing, isn't it, my boy? In such surroundings, associated with the infallibility of your surgical experts, all your primitive fears are laid to rest. Now this—" Dammy's host punched another button, and an assembly resembling a morgue slab under attack by a week's production of a cutlery factory deployed from the wall. "This is the automed, a masterpiece of ingenuity, adaptable to a vast variety of life-forms, including your own—and entirely physical-based, you understand. No subjective input required, making possible its use with subaware forms, luckily. Just stretch out here, and we'll soon have you right as rain."

"Where's the nurse?" Dammy demanded, hanging back.

"Ah, yes, the presence of a nubile female of your species would be useful to inspire a show of manly stoicism."

"Skip it," Dammy muttered. He was beginning to feel dizzy and weak. The warm, numb feeling in his side was wearing thin, allowing the sharp edges of something beneath to jab at his vitals in a tentative way.

Xorialle's hand swam out of the gathering mist to grip Montgomerie's arm. He allowed himself to be led forward, was vaguely aware of lying down on his back, of the touch of metal—not cold, but at body heat.

Then blackness as soft as soot and cobwebs folded down on him and blanketed out all thought. . . .

Two

This time his awakening was more leisurely. He lay for a while savoring the sensation of crisp sheets and a soft mattress, aware of the scent of broiling bacon and percolating coffee—a general feeling of utter well-being. Then his sense of reality rallied.

Yeah, I'm probably lying on my back in that alley with a slug in my skull dreaming all this, like I dreamed the little guy with the magic airplane and the carnation in his buttonhole. My best bet is to just lie easy and not make a wave and hold onto the hallucination as long as I can, because when it wears off . . .

"Awake, I see," a cheery, elderly voice spoke close at hand. Xorialle stood beside the bed casually attired in a lemon yellow terry-cloth jacket and shorts, a large Gene Autry watch with a wide yellow plastic band on his skinny wrist.

"Hey," Dammy said weakly, "you're real. . . ."

"We've already been over that," the old fellow said with a touch of severity, "as you know quite well. But I suppose it reassures you periodically to reinforce your self-image of nongullibility."

"How did . . . the operation go?"

"Why, as programmed, of course. Why do you ask? You feel well, I assume?"

"Not too bad," Dammy said weakly.

"I thought we'd start the day with a swim," Xorialle said briskly. "Not only refreshing, but a useful opportunity to assess just what it is I have to work with, coordination and endurance-wise."

"Are you kidding?" Dammy said with a break in his voice. "I'm good for at least two weeks flat on my back with radio music, artificial flowers, meals in bed, and pillow-fluffing once an hour."

"Yes, I'm sure you'd find those rituals comforting; but unfortunately time is of the essence. I'm sure you're rational enough to dispense with some of your traditional ceremonials."

"Ceremonials, my Uncle Gertrude! I've been shot and sliced open and sewed up, and the Confederate cavalry wouldn't get me out of this bed for at least, say, ten days!"

"Tsk. Old ideas *do* die hard. Pull up your nightshirt, Damocles, and examine your wound."

"Skip it. I can't even watch when I get a vaccination."

"See here, my boy, you have to make some minimal effort to discount the purely instinctive element in your behavior. Kindly do as I request."

"Or you'll give me an ulcer, I guess," Dammy said sullenly; but he complied with instructions. The smooth hide over his ribs was unmarred by so much as a mole.

"Uh . . . I guess it was the other side," he said, and pulled the garment away to expose a matching expanse of unblemished skin on the left.

"Well?" Xorialle said with studied patience. "I trust you're satisfied?"

Montgomerie rubbed his chin ruefully. "That was the realest dream I ever had," he said. "I would have sworn I took a slug in the short ribs, walked two blocks, got ambushed in an alley, and—well, after that it gets kind of silly." He managed a wry smile. "So maybe I've been working too hard. The laugh's on me." The smile faded, metamorphosed into a frown. "Either I've gone nuts, or all this is really happening. If I'm nuts, I'll be the last to know. So I might as well act as if everything is just the way it looks."

"Come, Damocles. Your pretense of imagining me to be a figure of fantasy wears thin. Accept the situation; don't fight the problem—solve it."

"Yeah. If I dreamed the whole thing, who does that make you? And how did I get here, wherever here is? And where's my clothes?"

"Suitable garments have been provided." Xorialle slid back a closet door to reveal a number of neat tunic-and-shorts outfits.

"I mean my real clothes. I can't go out of here in a pink kimono."

"I suspected the items would have emotional attachments. They've been cleaned and repaired and placed in your permanent quarters."

Dammy threw back the light blanket, walked to the curtained window, and looked out. A vista of blue-black ocean, white-flecked, stretched to the far horizon. There was nothing else in view.

"I'm really here—at the North Pole—and you really patched a hole in my side without even a scar?"

"That's more or less correct, Damocles."

"How long was I out? I'll bet I've been under

drugs for a couple months while you did plastic surgery, or . . ."

"Approximately seven hours and twenty-five minutes—since the repairs to your liver, that is."

"Nobody heals that fast," Dammy said without conviction.

"You did," Xorialle pointed out. "And while you were comatose, I gave you a thorough purging. You're healthier than you've ever before been in your life. Come along; I'll show you around the place. I think you'll find it interesting."

It was a spacious oak-paneled lounge with a magnificent view of the Arctic Sea. Wall shelves were filled with books; there were low tables and big soft chairs, handsome paintings on the walls. Double doors at one side opened into a dining room complete with long mahogany table and side-board, crystal chandelier, ornately carved chair-backs, and silver candelabras. The kitchens lay beyond—a symphony of gleaming stainless steel and pale yellow cabinet tops, bright with sunlight and potted flowers.

"Class," Dammy acknowledged. "Where's the hired help?"

"I have no servants; none are needed. All necessary functions are performed automatically."

"You live here alone?"

"I'm not affected by such problems as loneliness or ennui, I'm happy to say." Montgomerie's host pointed out the pantry, its shelves well stocked with familiar canned and bottled goods, its capacious freezers loaded with meats and fruits.

"None of this is essential, of course," he conceded. "The foodstuffs might more efficiently be stored out of sight or, more logically, synthesized as needed; but it amuses me to live in native style—and, of course, I was expecting a guest."

"Guest, huh? Funny, I don't remember getting an invitation."

"Dammy, kindly don't attempt to dramatize the situation by imagining sinister overtones. I've shown you nothing but kindness; I tended your hurts, you can't deny. Just relax and let's be friends."

"OK, doc. Shake." Xorialle took Montgomerie's proffered hand.

They descended a handsome spiral staircase to the level below, which was given over to offices and what looked like small classrooms, each equipped with specialized apparatus of curious design.

"Training aids," Xorialle explained succinctly. "You'll be seeing more of this soon."

The next level was devoted to sound-muffled rooms with capacious chairs, racks of what appeared to be tape cassettes, film reels, and other objects, of unfamiliar shape.

"The library and data facilities are as complete as any outside Data Central," Xorialle said with a note of pride, "and are updated continuously with inputs both from local sources and, ah, others."

"A library with no books," Dammy said. "It's a switch. What's that?" He pointed to a small hooded apparatus occupying a niche of its own. Adjacent to it were vertical channels in which glossy half-inch cubes were stacked like gum in a dispensing machine.

"Foreign-language technical data of no interest to you," Xorialle said shortly. "Don't take offense, my boy," he added sternly, "but on no account must you tamper with this section. I emphasize:

off-limits, Dammy. Don't touch! If you wish anything to read, my boy, you'll find it here," he concluded more mildly, and led Montgomerie across to an alcove with a row of buttons above a frosted glass plate.

"All your familiar literary treasures are here, from *The Wind in the Willows* to the *Congressional Record,* current as of this afternoon's session. Merely select from the catalog—" He pressed a button and a list of titles appeared on the screen, moving downward with increasing speed as he twisted a control knob—"and the work will be either projected here, or a copy produced for your use." He poked buttons, the machine whirred softly, and a handsomely bound copy of *Forever Amber* dropped from a slot.

Dammy grunted.

A small elevator took them to the level below. There were no windows here. Narrow corridors led between blank walls, ending at massive doors.

"Utility functions are handled here," Xorialle explained. "The various units are sealed and perform their functions, including self-repair, without supervision."

"Where's your power plant?"

Xorialle shot Dammy a thoughtful look. "Below," he said. "A small fusion cell using sea water."

"Let's take a look."

"I'm sorry. Off-limits. Radiation, you know. Well, that's about it, my boy. Shall we go up?"

"Quite a layout, doc. It must have cost some real bread to hollow out the whole rock and pack it full of machinery."

"The project hasn't been without expense," Xorialle agreed.

"What's it all for?"

"Later, my boy, later."

Back in the lounge, Xorialle dialed for drinks, which promptly slid into place on the bar. The wind had risen; it boomed against the wide glass areas, transmitting a feel of chill in spite of the comfortable temperature of the luxurious room.

"What happens when a blizzard hits?" Dammy said. "This place sticks up like a cherry on a sundae. These Arctic winds top a hundred and eighty, I heard someplace."

"Have no fear, my boy. The structure has withstood the weather for over three hundred years; I'm sure it will serve as long as it's needed."

"Air conditioning and all, huh?" Dammy glanced sideways at his host. "Pretty fancy for the seventeenth century."

"Don't trouble your head, my boy," Xorialle said offhandedly. "It will all be made clear in due course."

Dammy sampled his drink.

"This place is more than just a little weekend hideaway, right?"

"Quite right."

"You're a funny guy, Doc. You don't say any more than you want to, do you?"

"Do you?"

"Not if I can help it." Montgomerie shook his head. He frowned at Xorialle. "Why'd you bring me here, Doc?"

"To save your life, of course, in the first instance."

"How'd you know my name?"

"Research."

"Why research me?"

Xorialle spread his hands appealingly. "There was nothing personal, my boy. I required a subject in the early adult years, of average endowments, one whose disappearance from his usual haunts would attract a minimum of notice. My survey turned up a number of possibilities. I selected you."

"For what?"

"As a test subject."

"You with the government?" Montgomerie frowned darkly.

"Not exactly."

"What kind of test?"

"Oh, a standard wide-band evaluation—in your case with the emphasis on potential, of course, since your exploitation of your most recent evolutionary quantum jump has hardly begun."

"Why is it every question I ask you just gives me more questions to ask?"

"May I offer a word of advice, lad? Don't bother your head at this point. As we go forward with your development . . ."

"What's that mean?"

"Why, merely that there would be no point in attempting an evaluation based on your present physical and mental condition. We already have your unfortunate culture as ample evidence of your kind's ineptitude at this stage in solving even the most elementary societal problems. What is of interest is the magnitude of the impact you may represent on the Galactic Consensus at your point of maturation."

"Look, would you do me a favor? Talk ordinary American?"

Xorialle waggled his hands in an exasperated

gesture. "I can't quite see what it is you find so difficult to grasp. Naturally, the Concensus monitors developments within the Tessasphere. When a new species emerges onto the psychostratum, it's necessary to assess its potentialities in order to determine what, if any, role it should be permitted in galactic affairs, and in what direction its development should be guided for optimum convergence with Concensual goals."

"That's what I mean," Montgomerie said. "It sounds kind of like American, but it doesn't seem to tell me much."

"Accordingly," Xorialle ploughed on, "an average specimen is selected and his innate abilities explored, thus supplying data on which to base extrapolative calculations."

"That word *specimen*—I thought that was something you gave the lab technician or stuck a pin through for your butterfly collection."

"Your simple language," Xorialle said sourly, "is rich in encumbering connotations. In this case you, my boy, are the specimen." He held up a hand to forestall Dammy's comment. "And by determining the extent of your latent capabilities, I acquire in microcosm a measure of your kind's potential destiny."

"What do you mean by 'my kind'?" Dammy said suspiciously. "Is that some kind of crack?"

"Your *kind*, my dear lad: your race, tribe, breed, species, call it what you will."

"You mean American?"

"American, Russian, Zulu, Indio—you're all minor substocks of *Homo sapiens*, as you so naively term yourselves."

"You talk," Dammy said carefully, eyeing Xorialle gingerly, "as if you weren't included."

"I suppose I should have made that point clear earlier," the old gentleman said with a sigh. "You're quite right, of course, Damocles. I am not human."

Dammy edged away from his host. "OK, so you're a Martian," he said. "Just don't get excited. Just keep calm—"

"I'm perfectly calm, I assure you," Xorialle said sharply. "And I am by no means a Martian. My world of origin is some hundred parsecs distant from your minor solar system."

"Sure, whatever you say." Dammy measured with his eyes the distance between them, shifting his weight unobtrusively.

"Don't," Xorialle said wearily. "After such a nice beginning, let's not degrade our relationship back to the lion-tamer level."

Dammy sucked in a breath and jumped—or, more correctly, he initiated the neural commands which ordinarily would have expressed themselves in a sharp intake of breath and a lithe spring. Instead, he sat unmoving on the same spot. Not a quiver of a muscle reflected the inner turmoil as his somatic indicators responded to the fact that nothing had happened. Then, very slowly, he fell sideways onto the floor.

"Sorry," Xorialle said. "I may have pinched a trifle too hard."

"Think nothing of it," Dammy said weakly, struggling to his hands and knees, which were suddenly filled with pins and needles. "I guess I'm not quite as healthy as I thought I was." He groped his way back to the chair, still experiencing the shocking sensation of the *touch* within his mind, the incredible invasion of his most personal inner *me* by what seemed in retrospect to be a hair-fine tendril which had groped tentatively, then abruptly gripped hard—and thrust *him* aside.

Now, as he sat staring glumly across at his host, he felt the alien presence release its grip and withdraw, leaving behind in Dammy's thoughts a new conceptualization of his mind, compartmented, complex, interconnected in curious ways. He wondered . . .

"See here, Damocles," Xorialle said kindly. "It's necessary for the success of my work that you accept the realities of the situation. I can't directly influence your intellectual processes excessively without damaging the very areas I hope to develop: I'm forced to rely on your own vestigial intelligence to perceive the wisdom of cooperation."

"Look," Dammy said wearily, "I don't know much, maybe, but I know Martians are little green men, not old gents with trick moustaches. If you were some kind of space monster, you'd have bug eyes, tentacles, stuff like that. You wouldn't look like the rich uncle in a late TV movie."

"Why not?" Xorialle inquired with raised eyebrows.

Dammy eyed him shrewdly. "If you came from outer space, Pops, an oyster would be a closer relative of mine than you are."

"Not applicable. The *Mollusca* occupy an entirely different ecological niche."

"Or a Hottentot," Dammy said. "Why don't you look like a Bushman or an Eskimo or maybe one of those Ayrabs with whiskers down to here?"

"Would you have found that reassuring?"

"What's that got to do with it?"

Xorialle sighed. "It's of the greatest importance that a rapport based on a valid interpersonal relationship be established between us. I naturally assumed a guise calculated to stir as few as possible of your hostility syndromes. By appearing as an elderly and affluent member of your own racial strain, I sought to lay to rest any antipathies due to skin coloration, hair texture, and the rest, while not arousing rivalries based on fancied sexual competitiveness or male dominance factors."

"You talk like you had some choice," Montgomerie said. "Most guys I know have to settle for what Mother Nature handed them."

Xorialle wagged his head in exasperation. "You're proving unexpectedly resourceful in avoiding acceptance of the facts," he said. "I'd planned to prepare you more gradually, but it appears I'll have to risk the shock on your nervous system somewhat prematurely."

"What shock to my nervous system?" Dammy inquired nervously. "Take it easy now, Doc; my crazy bone is still twanging like a guitar from your last demonstration."

"The shock of seeing me as I actually am."

"I'm looking at you right now," Dammy said.

"Damocles—I'm in costume," Xorialle said gently.

"So? I've seen fake whiskers before. . . ."

"It's more than the hirsute appendages."

"OK, a putty nose, tinted contacts—" He broke off as Xorialle sighed and pressed a point behind his ear. A line appeared, bisecting his face from forehead to chin, running down his neck to disappear beneath the beach jacket. The fissure widened; his face opened like the two halves of a clamshell, exposing something gray-scaled, dull-gleaming inside.

"Have I made my point clear?" Xorialle's voice issued from the gaping orifice.

Dammy closed his eyes tight and said, "Close it up, close it up, close it up—"

"Very well; you may look now," Xorialle said in a more kindly tone. Montgomerie opened one eye. The old gentleman smiled at him amiably, looking perfectly normal now.

"By the way, Pop, what's it like out there—you know, in the stars and all?"

"I presume you intend to inquire as to conditions in extraterrestrial environments."

"Sure, that's what I said. I mean, how is it out there on Mars and stuff?"

"Damocles," the alien said sternly, "I must caution you that you are to make no effort to acquire data regarding the Concensus. The less you know of such matters, the better for you."

"Cripes, par me, Doc. I didn't mean to step on your corns."

"Any, ah, *other* questions?" Xorialle inquired gently.

"Not, ah, at this time," Dammy said dazedly.

"Splendid. I have a feeling this may turn out to be a most interesting evaluation after all," Xorialle said in a tone of satisfaction. "And now, shall we rest a bit? And tomorrow, on to your testing."

"Point me toward the bedroom and I'll take it from there," Dammy said, "No lessons needed."

Xorialle escorted him to a handsomely appointed chamber and switched on a soft light which illuminated a fawn-colored carpet, pale gold walls, a handsome oak bedstead with a charcoal and chocolate spread, matching chairs and drapes at the wide (false?) windows.

"Sleep well, my boy," Xorialle said benignly. He nodded and left him with a cheery good-night.

Lying in the darkness, Dammy waited five minutes. Then he rose silently and tried the door. It was locked. He frowned thoughtfully and returned to his bed.

Well, Damocles thought, *I don't know. Swell place, and the old boy—or whatever he is—has treated me right, just like he said. But sticking his fingers in my brains like he did gives me the galloping willies. Well, I guess I can worry about that in the morning. . . .*

On a sudden impulse he rose and went to the closet. His clothes—not Xorialle's issue outfits—hung there, clean and pressed. Further back in the far corner of the roomy closet hung another garment. Danny examined it—a knee-length coat of coarse blue cloth, with brass buttons and mixed-up lapels. The back-of-the-neck part stood up and folded back in a soft roll, while the lower part lay flat.

Looks like the last guy who stayed here dressed like George Washington, Danny mused. *But Xorialle said I was the only one ever slept in this room. Funny, a guy lying when there's no reason for it. There's more to old Al than he lets on. . . .*

Dammy took the flat leather tool kit from a concealed pocket of the blazer he had worn the night he was shot—or not shot. He checked it quickly; everything was there. Either Xorialle had missed it or he hadn't looked. Maybe the old boy missed a bet once in a while after all. . . .

Three

It was almost midnight, eight days later. Dammy slumped in a large and handsome contour chair upholstered in glove-soft ocher leather, gazing across the wide and beautifully appointed lounge toward the wall of glass affording the spectacle of the sun that hung on the horizon, dyeing the sky and sea crimson and purple.

"Well, it's been a busy week," Xorialle said briskly from his perch on a large violet ottoman before the cheery blaze that crackled on the tiled hearth. "But not without result—though there does seem to be a remarkably potent otiosity factor that needs to be compensated for in my calculations."

"That gym," Dammy groaned. "And those flashing lights, and that buzz machine. I don't know whether my head or my back aches worst."

"Worse," Xorialle said. "Precision of diction is vital to accurate communication. As for your imagined pains—dismiss them. They're no more than self-induced tensions."

"You and your torture machines are what induced them, along with the blisters and the spots before my eyes. This is a lousy way to treat an invalid in his first week out of bed."

"Don't fret, Damocles," Xorialle said comfortably. "We've managed to exercise most of your physical and mental faculties sufficiently to give me the bulk of the data I require at present." He frowned thoughtfully. "Frankly, I'm rather surprised. Your nervous system seems to be a very fine instrument indeed, though largely unused, of course. And your physical condition is not at all bad for a specimen whose development has been random, undirected. That's not too surprising, actually; the ideal psychosome, after all, is one perfectly adapted to its environment, and a natural environment will produce a normal animal. Your somewhat irregular habits of life have introduced sufficient variety into your activities to preclude any premature deterioration such as results from a sedentary or overly specialized life style."

"I could have told you I keep in shape; I work out a couple times a week—"

"Please, my boy," Xorialle said tiredly. "No chest beating just now. I have the data; anecdotal emendations are quite superfluous."

Montgomerie brightened. "Well, that's something. In that case, I guess you'll be running me back to town in the morning." He waved a hand at the room. "They'll never believe me when I tell them about this setup," he said almost cheerfully. "A luxury penthouse, only more so, a few thousand miles from anywhere. You must have a couple million bucks worth of equipment in the lab and the gym and the kitchen, plus this fancy furniture, the power plant—"

"Ah—Dammy," Xorialle began, but Montgomerie

chattered on: "And I'll get a real lift out of the look on Chico's face when he sees me. But on the other hand," he went on more soberly, "I might be smarter to just fade out like Jeannie said and pick a new hometown."

"Damocles," Xorialle cut in, "I'm afraid you've leaped to a faulty conclusion. I won't be running you back in the morning—"

"Oh, tonight, huh? Well, OK. But I was kind of looking forward to another good snooze in that bedroom. I'll give you that, Doc—you've got good mattresses, and the chow is all right too—"

"I'm glad you approve," the old gentleman broke in, "because you'll be enjoying them for some time to come."

Dammy sat up and frowned darkly. "Hey, look," he said. "You been running me ragged all week swinging on ropes and jumping hurdles and holding my breath and marking X's on charts and picking out things that matched and things that didn't match, and memorizing telephone numbers, and I've had it! I'm pooped. I'm not going through another day like this one—I don't care if you plant a blowtorch in my duodenum!"

"Where did you learn that word?"

"I read a few of your books, you know," Dammy said sullenly.

"Well . . . you continue to surprise me."

Dammy was on his feet now. "This is a free country. You got no right to hold a man prisoner."

"Odd, I'd gathered the impression you were contemptuous of your tribal taboo structure. But no matter; I assure you I am in no way bound by local custom. My duties require that I act in the best interest of the Concensus, regardless of possible inconvenience to you; surely you see that?"

"I'm leaving in the morning, Doc, and that's final."

"How?"

"Well . . ." Dammy faltered. "Well, blast it, Doc, it's up to you to get me back! Kidnapping is a federal rap!"

"I saved your life," Xorialle pointed out patiently. "I propose only to make use of a segment of your existence which would have been eliminated but for my intervention."

"You said you were finished. What more do you want out of me?"

"My dear boy, I've completed the preliminary calibration of your body and brain, an inventory of your equipment, so to speak."

"Yeah?"

"Tomorrow the real work begins."

"What work?"

"Training you, of course—as I explained at the beginning."

"Training me how?"

"In every way." Xorialle spread his hands as if stating the obvious.

"You mean—like Certified Public Accountancy and TV Repair?"

"All that, my lad—and much, much more."

"I don't get it, Doc. I didn't apply for night school or answer an ICS ad or sign up for on-the-job training. I've got a high school diploma, for crying into your malted milk! Where'd you get the idea I was on a self-improvement kick?"

"Not you, Damocles. Me."

"Oh, *you're* Training for a Big Pay Job in Radio. I get it."

"I mean," Xorialle said with precision, "that I intend to develop your every innate faculty to its highest possible potential, to explore every latent talent and ability of your psychosome."

Montgomerie sank back down in the chair.

"Latent," Dammy repeated hesitantly. "That means like what maybe I could do if I tried, only I never tried?"

"Approximately that."

"Like, uh, judo, karate," Dammy said thoughtfully. "Stuff like that?"

"At the beginning we'll acquire the rudimentary techniques already current in your extant embryonic cultures," Xorialle agreed. "Then, of course, we'll move on to totally unexplored areas." He rubbed his hands together briskly. Dammy wondered for a fleeting moment if they were real hands or prosthetics with tentacles curled inside them.

"That's the portion of the work that I find most fascinating, of course," Xorialle continued. "One sometimes discovers quite unexpected capabilities stored away in the genes of the most unlikely organism, waiting to be called forth by circumstance. As for example the Yling of Krako 88, a mud-dwelling species equipped with sonar-type sensory organs, who, if developed, were capable, with training, of direct null-time star communication using the same organs in another mode—a most useful skill, which would have remained forever undiscovered had not one of their number been gathered in by a Concensual sampling team."

"You mean you figure to train me to be some kind of teletype operator?"

Xorialle sighed in exasperation. "Certainly not, Damocles, as I'm sure you realize. These attempts to evade recognition of facts by simplistic verbalizations do you no credit. What your own hidden aptitudes might be, I as yet have little idea. But we'll discover them. Have no doubt of that."

"I took a test once," Dammy said thoughtfully, "that was supposed to tell me what career to go into. It said I had a rare talent for hotel management. But it was a hotel management school that gave the test, so maybe that had something to do with it."

"My assessment will probe far deeper," Xorialle stated, placing his (imitation?) fingertips together. "In effect, we'll telescope the next five or ten thousand years of your species' niche-exploration and cultural development into a matter of days."

"Hold it, Doc! If you think you're going to turn me into one of those guys with a bulgy head and little bitty arms and legs, you got a couple new thinks coming!"

"Damocles, don't be silly. My mission is exploration of the species, not forced evolution. I have no intention of inducing mutation, either along the lines of the laughable stereotype you postulate or any other. I'll simply train you, not change you. A girl who learns shorthand and typing is the same girl; a man who memorizes a poem or masters chess is the same man."

"What was all that about telescoping ten thousand years?" Dammy demanded.

Xorialle shook his head. "Let's not get things out of order, Damocles. First we'll see to it that you absorb the techniques and abilities already possessed by members of your race—then on to new areas. I should like to begin at once, but I suppose you feel you must sleep first?" He eyed Dammy questioningly. The latter yawned.

After a dreamless night, Damocles met Xorialle at the breakfast table.

"Memory," Xorialle said, "is basic to all learning. We will therefore begin today by perfecting your memory."

It was a dazzling morning, though the light streaming past the curtains was artificial. Master and pupil sat in a breakfast nook at a small table bright with a checkered cloth and colored dishes, beside windows from which the curtains were drawn back on a view of a sunny garden under an all but invisible dome. Dammy took another swallow of his second cup of coffee and patted his belt line comfortably.

"My memory's OK, Doc," he said. "Don't worry about that part."

"Indeed? What did you have for breakfast on the eight hundred and twenty-first day of your life? Or last October ninth, for that matter?"

"How do I know?"

"Under hypnosis you'd recall quite clearly. The data are there, my lad—merely inaccessible. The training will consist of improved indexing and retrieval procedures." Xorialle touched a button, and the table cleared itself swiftly and soundlessly.

Dammy looked dubiously at his host.

"Memory is a complex function," Xorialle stated musingly. "Without delving into the details of its function, consider merely the mechanism. Data impinge on your sensory receptors, are relayed to the brain. Some are stored, some held for ready use, others are shunted to the subconscious, some few are discarded. The factor by which the discrimination is made I call 'interest.' Obviously, if you attempted consciously to record every detail of every passing moment, you'd be faced with impossible overload conditions. At this very moment you're ignoring the bulk of the impressions pouring into your brain—after first assessing them, of course. A sleeping man pays no attention to the clamor of vehicles passing a few feet from his window, but a single creak of a supposedly locked bedroom door will rouse him at once. Waking, your mind performs the same filtering function, not only on what is to be noted, but what is to be stored."

"Sure, but—"

"Most of what I'm now saying, for example, is being shunted to dead storage by your brain, since it doesn't interest you. Any child who has ever been forced to memorize the multiplication table is aware of the reluctance of the brain to absorb at a conscious level data which the unreasoning discrimination center says are valueless. Unhappily, the discriminator was evolved to serve the needs of an animal who had no use for arithmetic. You may attempt to flog your reluctant brain on to more effective memorization by telling it that the upcoming exam is vital to your career, but the primitive brain knows nothing of these matters.

"Contrarily, data which are of obvious and immediate interest are remembered instantly, painlessly. Any baseball fan, however dull scholastically, can report at once the status of a game he's watching: inning, score, strike and ball count, team league standing, batting averages, and so on. A child can follow the identities of the characters and the story lines of dozens of comic strips simultaneously, picking up each one after a twenty-four hour lapse with no difficulty—although he may be totally unable to remember the incidents recounted in a history text."

"So kids like the funnies," Dammy said. "So what?"

"The mind erects barriers to reject the superfluous data—the 'uninteresting' data. Only repetition can penetrate those barriers to cut a retrieval path. With the catalyzer, I place the discriminator under your conscious control. Simple?"

"Like a Chinese menu. Will it hurt?"

"You play cards?" Xorialle inquired casually, producing a deck from somewhere in the sleight-of-hand fashion that Dammy had begun to accept as Xorialle's normal manner rather than an attempt to impress him.

"A little five-card stud now and then. None of that spit-in-the-ocean garbage."

Xorialle shuffled the cards with deft movements of his slender fingers and snapped the top card face up on the table.

"Call it," he said.

"Four of clubs."

"Four of clubs," Xorialle echoed, and turned a second card. It was the ten of diamonds. Dammy said so. Xorialle exposed a third card.

"Hey, I know a spade from a club, if that's what's worrying you," Dammy protested. "And I count like a champ, all the way up to a hundred—"

"Call it," Xorialle said patiently.

"Queen of spades."

"Queen of spades." Xorialle turned the cards

one at a time until he had run through the entire deck. He picked up the stack and turned it over, paused with his fingers on the top card, and looked inquiringly at Dammy.

"Come, my boy," he said sharply as Montgomerie stared back at him. "Let us not waste time with rituals. You know something is expected of you. Anticipate my verbalization."

"I'm supposed to tell you what the first card is?" Dammy guessed indifferently. "It was the four of clubs, unless you gave me a fast shuffle."

Xorialle turned over the four of clubs and waited, fingers poised over the second card.

"Uh, the uh, ten of, uh, diamonds."

Xorialle turned the card.

"And the queen of spades," Dammy continued. He called seven cards correctly in sequence before he went blank.

"Not too bad for a first attempt," Xorialle said, folding the deck as soon as Dammy had missed.

"Hold it; keep going," Montgomerie said. "I didn't know I was that good. I can—"

"You've broken the gestalt, the association of each card with the one following. Your calls from this point on will be virtually random, meaningless."

"Let's try that again. I wasn't really concentrating."

The old gentleman gave Dammy a small smile. "Quite exciting, isn't it? Discovering a new ability, I mean. That's what makes life so endlessly stimulating to the very young. Every day they explore their capabilities, discovering facts about themselves. A small boy will sometimes jump into water to *see* if he can swim, or off a roof to learn if flying is included in his innate skills. He's quite used to such discoveries regarding his own strength, social dominance, whistling ability, and so on. As the years pass, such discoveries become rarer. You, for example, know very well you can't ride a horse or pilot an airliner. You know your place in the social pecking order and the sexual competition. Still, you continue to hope for glad surprises to greet you as you go through your days. It's that factor which makes giveaway contests so popular, sends people to palm readers and astrologers for news of unsuspected talents, makes the unwrapping of birthday presents so important a part of the ritual. Always there lurks the unvoiced hope that somehow under the wrappings lies a wonderful secret—about yourself."

"All that from a deck of cards?"

Xorialle ignored the question, swung a small table out in front of Montgomerie, and placed the deck of cards on it.

"Have you ever been hypnotized, Damocles?"

"No. I don't believe in that psychic stuff."

"Tsk. The hypnotic capacity is as normal and commonplace as the ability to sleep—and a good example of an innate capacity that went undiscovered by its possessors until recent years. Rather than chanting formulae, I intend to directly stimulate the portion of your brain normally reached by such methods. Just relax . . ." He returned to the console and touched buttons. Dammy felt a high, faint singing somewhere behind his eyes. The room seemed to change subtly, strike a new balance, become somehow more alive, more immediate than before.

"Turn the first card, my boy." Xorialle's voice

had a strange, faraway but compelling quality. Montgomerie turned the card.

"Three of spades," he said dreamily.

"Continue."

One by one, he went through the fifty-two cards.

"Shuffle," Xorialle said.

Dammy shuffled the deck.

"For each card of this next run which you call correctly, a magnificent prize awaits you," the old gentleman said solemnly. At once Dammy felt his heart accelerate. His mouth felt dry. Visions of incredible luck flashed before his eyes. He turned the cards quickly; their patterns seemed vivid, meaningful. He finished. . . .

"That's all," Xorialle said. "Revert to normal awareness."

It was as though an impalpably fine mesh gauze dropped over the scene. For a moment, Dammy had a sense of dullness, of numbness. The feeling faded.

"Call the first run," Xorialle said.

Dammy reached for the deck.

"Never mind that," Xorialle said curtly. "Just visualize them."

"Three of . . . spades," Dammy said. He called two more, then drew a blank.

"Call the second run," Xorialle ordered.

Instantly the mental image of a card snapped into focus. He called the entire deck as rapidly as he could speak.

"Start again with the twelfth card."

Dammy reeled them off.

"Call them in reverse."

Dammy did it.

"Add three to each number, call face cards in

reverse rank, and shift suits in the order spades, hearts, clubs, diamonds."

Dammy recited as required with no loss of speed.

"So much for memory, my lad," Xorialle said brightly. "Your key symbol for total recall is *three of spades*. And by the way, while I was about it, I established a self-hypnotic trigger you can employ when needed. Key word: *prize*."

"How," Dammy said in wonderment, "did I do that?"

"Tell me, could you have memorized the deck, left to your own devices?"

"Sure—I guess—if I went through it a couple dozen times."

"I employed the same process—lubricated a trifle. How many song lyrics do you know?"

"Who, me? I don't go in for—"

"Such effeminate pursuits. I know. Nevertheless, you've heard the words of certain popular tunes over and over; some of them have lodged in your mind. The average man, if pressed, could recite some dozens of them. Suppose each song includes one hundred words, each word keyed to a distinct note of the scale. Each word in turn consists of an average of six letters. If a message were to be encoded to those letters using sequence and pitch to carry additional intelligence, a considerable amount of information could be transmitted, do you agree?"

"Well, I . . ."

"Word order itself is a powerful tool. Consider the difference between 'travel time' and 'time travel.' And punctuation: 'This book was dictated by God,' versus 'This book was dictated, by God!' "

"Uh, yeah, but . . ."

"From now on we'll make use of that waste capacity. Now—let's get on with the refurbishing of your concentration, computational ability, deductive faculties, pattern perception, and so on. The sooner we finish the preliminaries, the sooner we can get into the substantive portion of the program."

Xorialle looked speculatively at his subject.

"Damocles, what is the most delightful experience in the world?"

"It's not yodeling a few bars in the shower and finding out I sound like Johnny Cash," Dammy said with a smirk.

"Be candid, lad."

Dammy leered. "I guess it's when a nice-looking chick falls for you out of a clear sky."

"Precisely. Why?"

Dammy spread his hands. "You need a diagram?"

Xorialle shook his head dismissingly. "It's not merely the prospect of sexual contact, my boy; in most cases some such outlet already exists. It is, rather, the flattering insight into yourself, the surprising and reassuring news that you possess unsuspected charms capable of so powerfully affecting another."

"Nuts, Doc, there's some things you'll never get out of a test tube, and savvying the romance schtick is one of 'em."

"No matter. We'll have ample time to turn up all your latent potencies later in the program. At the moment, we're concerned with basics. Come along." He rose.

"I don't know if I'm going along any farther with this training course of yours," Montgomerie growled, keeping his seat. "What's in it for me?"

Xorialle sighed. "Damocles, do you have any idea how much time and effort are wasted in acting out rituals designed to dramatize attitudes which in most cases are nonexistent—mere bows to convention?"

"Doc, give me a break; talk plainer," Dammy said sarcastically.

"You feel it's incumbent on you to pretend to a reluctance to cooperate with me; this in turn springs from the need to maintain the facade of an independent, self-determining, dominant male. So you propose to engage me in a symbolic conversation in which I slowly overcome your objections by acceptable means such as cajolery, appeals to your curiosity and gratitude, and so on. And of course you feel compelled to pretend skepticism of my statements in order not to appear gullible—just as a yokel, captivated by the chromium decorations on a used car, will attempt to dissemble from the glib salesman his lust to buy, pretending indifference even as he signs the papers, lest he seem an easy mark; and as a woman will pretend to discourage the advances of a male she has already decided to accept, in order not to appear overly compliant."

"You sure cover a lot of ground, Doc," Dammy said in mock admiration. "From card tricks to chicks that play hard to get. What's this got to do with me learning judo and how to live to be three thousand?"

"Learn to know yourself, lad," Xorialle said sadly. "Acknowledge that your charade of confident cynicism covers the fact that you're quite intrigued by the prospects before you."

"Try me!" Montgomerie barked. "Drop me back

in Chi, and see how far I chase you begging for another chance."

"Yes, you're quite capable of turning your back on what lies before you, in order to maintain your role—like a stoic proud of his reputation for abstinence spurning the food he needs and desires."

"You're saying I *want* to be locked inside this ice palace with a frustrated college professor, memorizing the spots on cards?" Montgomerie snorted. "Doc, if you only knew—"

"What sort of life did you lead outside, Damocles? A hand-to-mouth existence of—" Xorialle smiled sadly—"nursing a secret belief in your unique superiority, waiting for the wonderful surprise that would one day come along to transform your life."

"Me? I'm not waiting for anything—"

But Xorialle had gone on. "The surprise has arrived, Dammy. In a way, you *were* unique. You happened to be the one individual whom I chose out of the billions—at random, true—as my subject. Now let's proceed without further ritualistic objection."

Xorialle turned and walked away. After a moment Montgomerie rose from the table and followed.

"This," Xorialle said, indicating a chair with a beehive-shaped apparatus hinged at the top, "is a synaptic catalyzer." He patted the device almost affectionately. "A rather crude field model, assembled from local components as is everything here. But effective. It will make our task infinitely simpler by speeding the normal learning process. Just take a seat, my boy, while I run a few calibration tests."

"It looks like a hair drier in a beauty shop,"

Montgomerie said disapprovingly. "If anybody saw me sitting under that—"

"I thought we agreed to dispense with the rituals. It's understood you're fulfilling the role of a virile male ready to fight for food or a mate, impatient of the effeminate. Sit down."

Dammy complied, with a show of reluctance. "You're going to flash slides on the wall, right, while I call off the answers?"

"I work directly with the cerebrum," Xorialle said absently, studying the dials on a small console behind which he had seated himself. "Initially I'll fire a battery of impulses through your cortex, note the results, and adjust the input profile accordingly."

"You're not scrambling *my* brains," Dammy said, rising quickly. Xorialle looked at him sadly.

"Dammy, scrambling your brain is, I assure you, very far from my intentions. I've gone to considerable trouble to procure a normal, healthy, untrained neural system to work with. The slightest tampering would destroy your usefulness to me."

"If running electricity through my head isn't tampering, I don't know what is!"

"That's correct; you don't. The catalyzer is analogous to the flashlight an oculist shines in your eye, testing, not destroying vision. Now kindly quell your superstitious fears and instinctive dreads and ritual objections and allow me to proceed."

Dammy muttered but made no further complaint as Xorialle lowered the dome over his head and returned to his console.

"Just sit quietly," he said. "The calibration will only take a few moments. It's quite painless, I assure you."

Dammy heard a soft buzz; voices seemed to clamor at the edge of hearing, but he felt nothing.

"You're not shooting X-rays through me?" he queried.

Xorialle gave an impatient grunt. "Neuronic vibrations identical with those produced by your own mentational field." He touched a key and the murmuring ceased. He twiddled knobs and levers, adjusted dials, frowning in concentration.

"Now," he said, "I think our next order of business is to do something about that grotesque dialect you speak. Grammar and syntax have a function in communication that appears to have escaped you." He fussed over his console.

"I don't like the sound of that," Dammy protested. "You going to make me talk like a college professor or something?"

"Or something," Xorialle mimicked. "A sterling example of the type of meaningless noise that clogs your speech. Quiet, now."

Dammy sat tensely. Something tickled his brain; a soft squeaking as of gossiping mice chattered between his ears. It went on and on while Dammy gazed down unguessed-of vistas suddenly revealed.

"Now." Xorialle's voice woke him from his reverie. "We should see a marked improvement. Say something, my boy."

"What do you wish me to say?" Dammy said promptly. "I mean, uh, sure, Doc. What about?"

"Don't fight the impulse to clear speech, Damocles. Tell me your impressions of the training thus far."

"The techniques appear highly sophisticated; I'll be unable to judge their effectiveness until I've gathered more data—" Montgomerie broke off and shook his head. "For crying into your soft-boiled eggs, Doc, you've impressed on me a speech pattern which will attract ridicule from my peer group—I mean damn it, I sound like a book! What was your intention—I mean what's the big idea?"

"There, there, calmly, my boy. Shall we proceed?"

"I have no option in the matter—I mean what does it matter what I think? You'll proceed in any event—I mean go ahead anyway!"

"Correct. Possibly you're learning a bit of wisdom after all, lad."

"Wisdom would have kept me clear of you in the first instance," Dammy said bitterly, "before you loused up my conversation."

"Tsk. Cynicism ill becomes you, my boy," Xorialle said with mock severity. "But let us proceed."

Four

Montgomerie spent five wearying hours under the catalyzer as Xorialle clucked, muttered, poked buttons, and issued cryptic instructions, lecturing the while. Afterward they lunched on pheasant and wine, served automatically on what seemed to be an open-air terrace. When they had finished, Xorialle handed a small book across to his pupil.

"*Hoyle's Complete Games,*" Dammy read aloud. "I thought we had work to do. When will we have time for pinochle?"

"Don't be tedious, Damocles. You'll learn games along with the rest, of course."

"The rest of what, Doc?" Dammy frowned. "When do we get to jujitsu and—"

"Dammy," Xorialle cut in sharply, "in the next few days you will master the rules and techniques of every activity, skill, talent, sport, and art ever mastered by any human being anywhere. Do I make myself clear? You will be as expert at chipping flints as at architectural drafting, as skilled at dominoes as at basket weaving. Able to juggle, walk a tightrope, and add the numerals on the sides of passing freight cars as fast as any idiot savant in the land. Understood?"

"Now I know you're ribbing me, Doc."

"My name is Xorialle! I am not a tribal shaman! I dislike the eke-name 'Doc'! I am not 'ribbing' you! And I'd appreciate it if you'd make use of your knowledge of your native language before I forget my mission here and—"

"And what?" Dammy challenged as his mentor broke off abruptly and went inside. Dammy followed.

Xorialle sighed. "Even your primitive tongue would be endurable if you used it correctly. You have complete knowledge of grammar, vocabulary, and syntax now. Why not make use of it?"

"Habit, I guess," Dammy said indifferently. "Or maybe I just don't want to sound like a nance."

"I know a solution," Xorialle said grimly. "You'll learn Concensual Two, a simple form of speedspeak."

"Hold it, Doc," Dammy demurred. "You said *human* skills, remember? I don't want any weird alien kind of stuff pumped into my brain."

"Nonsense. C-2 is designed for interspecies communication and is as free of specialized bias as the concept of language permits. It won't warp your personality any more than a knowledge of Navaho would."

"What's it sound like?" Danny asked anxiously as his tutor settled the catalyzer in place.

Xorialle made a scraping noise with his tongue and hard palate.

"That was Lincoln's Gettysburg Address. I confess it loses something in translation." He busied himself at the controls.

"Relax, blank your mind," he ordered curtly. Dammy leaned back in the chair and closed his eyes. Abruptly a voiceless clamor started up somewhere behind his ears. It went on and on. He dozed. . . .

". . . enumerate from unity to 1010," Xorialle was saying.

Dammy drew a deep breath and let it out. With an effort he suppressed his tongue's impulse to twitch, keeping his jaws clamped hard.

"What sszzzrrchhh happenezzchhh?" he said.

Xorialle buzzed. A meaning seemed to want to attach to the sound, but Dammy shunted it aside.

"That made my head achesssdzzz," Dammy said. "Well, when do I zzsstart to speakrrrxx . . ." He paused. "My tongue feelzzz xxrfunny. Funny, I mean. My . . . tongue . . . feels . . . funny." He enunciated distinctly. "What did you do, Doc, louse up my talk box?"

"Xxxrrssszzzkk," Xorialle buzzed. "Bbyrrppp?"

"Say 'excuse me,' " Dammy muttered.

"You don't understand me?"

"You sound like a bluefly in a beer bottle."

"This is *very* strange; I was sure you had the capacity. Well, even negative data are data. A pity I don't have a master analyzer here; I'd like to get to the bottom of the anomaly. But it's outside my actual program in any case. Never mind. We'll continue in English—but do try to speak more precisely, there's a good lad. Now where were we?"

"You were talking about juggling," Dammy reminded him.

"And human fly work, steeplejacking, body surfing, skydiving, scuba diving." Xorialle paused for breath. "Acrobatics, pole vaulting, lariat throwing, qualitative analysis, lens grinding, Wankel engine repair, tennis, skittles, curling, ballet—"

"Ballet!"

"Everything, Dammy."

"That's impossible," Dammy gulped, "even if I'd go along with it."

Xorialle's expression tightened. "If?"

Dammy felt a sharp twinge in his chest. It was just a tiny, glowing ember of pain, but it held steadily.

"If?" Xorialle repeated.

"All right, all right, what choice have I got?" Dammy gasped in relief as the spark went out.

"As for the impossibility of the program, do you deny that somewhere someone is expert in any given human specialty?"

Dammy grunted assent.

"What one man can do, another can do."

"But not all at once, for crying into your Alka-Seltzer!"

"Why not?"

"It takes a guy years just to learn to deal black-jack! And they say scientists spend twenty years in college these days and then can't keep up with the new stuff coming up!"

"But you'll learn more quickly than they, Damocles. Open the book in your hand."

Montgomerie flipped the pages, stopped at one headed EUCHRE LAWS.

"Key words," Xorialle snapped.

Dammy started to comply, but the oldster cut him off.

"Subvocalize!"

Dammy thought, *Three of spades . . . prize.*

"Look at the page." The words hung in the air like solid objects.

Dammy glanced at the close print.

"Riffle the pages."

"Dammy complied, glancing at the blur of swiftly turning leaves.

"Close the book."

He closed the book.

"Recite."

Dammy opened his mouth to object—" 'If any player names the suit already turned down, he loses his right to name a suit; and if he corrects himself and names another, neither he nor his partner is allowed to make that suit the trump.' "

"You now know," Xorialle said severely, "the rules of euchre. It remains to absorb the strategies of actual play."

"OK, so I memorized a couple lines," Dammy said. "What about the other four hundred pages?"

"You know them," Xorialle said complacently.

"So what will that make me—a cardsharper? I've got bigger ideas than that, Doc."

"You won't stop there. You'll absorb all the information in all the books—your race's entire heritage of knowledge."

Dammy snorted. "Even flipping pages like riffling a deck, I couldn't get through all the books there are in a lifetime."

"Oh, you'll use the tapes, of course. The viewer will project them at high speed as soon as we've coaxed your scanning rate up to a reasonable figure. You'll be able to absorb the *Britannica*, for example, in about eighty seconds."

"Look, I'm no supergenius, Doc; my brains won't hold it all."

"How many days has August, Damocles?"

"Ah, thirty days hath September," Dammy murmured, "April, June, November . . . thirty-one," he announced.

"You see? The datum was there, but encoded. We will encode a great deal more information."

"If I stop and recite a poem every time I want to remember something, they'll lock me up in the chuckle ward," Dammy objected.

"Our codes will be simpler and our retrieval much faster," Xorialle reassured him. "Now, off to bed with you, lad. Tomorrow we'll be taking up the physical portion of the program, and I want you fresh and full of vigor."

"Yeah," Dammy said, yawning. "Good idea."

In bed, Dammy stretched luxuriously, then scratched at a small but persistent itch behind his right ear. The spot was tender, slightly swollen. He fingered it, trying to recall . . . *three of spades.*

. . . a fading pain in his abdomen, the pull of new stitches there, then the ghostly sensation of the scalpel against the mastoid process, the remote vibration of the bone drill; then Xorialle's deft fingers slipping the control device into place to extrude its semiliving organometallic filament which followed the auditory nerve to the cortex, whence it elaborated into a network invading every portion of his cerebrum. Curiously he examined the structure, using hitherto unused senses and organs of introspection to trace leads, analyze circuits, and study receptors. So doing, he glimpsed the fantastic complexity not only of the invading filamentary network, but of his own mind. Phantom perceptors and manipulators lay unused in his

brain. The alien network ended, but Dammy went on. . . . Gradually, probing gingerly along newly discovered pathways, he began to grasp the dynamic symmetry of the fantastic structure that was his mind. Then he blinked and turned his thoughts to more mundane matters.

So the old devil was lying about that, too, when he pretended to be using pure mental control to stab my gizzard and freeze me stiff, he ruminated. *I wonder what he's really up to? . .*

He rose, got his tool kit from the closet, then went to the door, squatted, and studied the tiny aperture beneath the latch. He selected a wire-thin instrument, inserted it, put his ear to the door, and slowly rotated the pick. There were faint clicks from the mechanism. Something *snick*ed with a more decisive sound. Dammy withdrew the tool and tried the latch. The door opened smoothly. He stepped out into the passage, went quickly to the stairs, descended to the library level. The lights were low in the Book Room. He went to the section devoted to Xorialle's off-world texts, selected half a dozen of the small cubes, dropped them into the feed tray of the scanner, and switched it on. The screen lit up. For an instant the pattern of close-packed dots seemed meaningless; then, abruptly, information was leaping at him from the page.

Three of spades, he subvocalized, and settled himself in the chair, his eyes on the screen . . . *prize.*

He blinked and sat up. His neck ached, his eyes burned. A glance at the clock showed that two hours had passed. The screen before him was blank. He switched it off, replaced the data cubes, and returned to his room. He slept quickly but had troubled dreams.

The small chamber to which Xorialle led Montgomerie next morning was windowless, with unadorned pale gray walls and ceiling. Its sole furnishing was a large assembly occupying the center of the floor, filling most of the available space. Dammy circled the latter as Xorialle bustled over to a corner to push one of his inevitable buttons, deploying a small desk-type console packed tight with more buttons.

"It looks," Dammy stated, "like a collision between a traction bed and a jungle gym, with a dentist's chair thrown in—from a third story window."

"The responder may not appear very impressive, my boy," the old fellow acknowledged, poking keys in a rapid sequence and staring assessingly at the resultant pattern of colored indicator lights. "In external appearance, at least. But it's a most ingenious apparatus capable of simulating the response of the immediate exocosm to your every movement, as well as applying carefully metered stimuli to your musculature."

"Translation?" Dammy requested automatically.

"Once fitted to you, with appropriate neural contacts, the responder will do a remarkable job of acting as trapeze, gravity field, fencing opponent, centrifuge—the entire gamut of external conditions and forces needed to exercise you in the disciplines we'll be covering."

"Jake. Now explain the translation—and to save time, maybe you could explain the explanation as you go along."

"More of your anti-intellectual pose, based on the proposition so popular among the unlettered that sagacity is unmanly," Xorialle dismissed his pupil's gibe. "Let's suppose you're learning fencing. The appropriate adjustments are made, and as you lunge, thrust, and parry, the responder will parry, thrust, and lunge in return—or the equivalent—with all the skill of a master of foil, sabre, and epee."

"What's peddling hot merchandise got to do with me living to a ripe old age?"

Xorialle waved the question away. "But at first, of course, we'll be busy for a time with honing your basic tools. Into the responder with you now, Damocles—there's a good lad."

"You want me to climb inside that Rube Goldberg?" As he spoke, the assembly stirred, seemed to fold in on itself, separating into two halves which opened wide, leaving a clear access to a system of rods and slings at its heart.

Xorialle merely sighed. Dammy clambered in, settled himself gingerly. The frame closed on him. Padded arms and feelers nudged him, nestling into position; clamps slid deftly into place, locking his arms, legs, torso, and head in contact with a maze of rods, straps, levers, wires. He fought down a surge of claustrophobia.

"Comfortable?" Xorialle called.

"Are you kidding?" Dammy replied in a muffled voice. "I'm wrapped up in hardware like a mummy!"

"Is your free movement restricted?" Xorialle sounded concerned. Montgomerie moved a finger tentatively. The attached apparatus moved soundlessly with it, without resistance. He flexed his arm, then a leg, moved his shoulders, twisted his head.

"Funny," he said. "I can't even feel the stuff."

"Stand up, please."

"How can I?" Dammy said, but when he stood the gear rode lightly with him.

"Run in place, swing your arms, jump up and down, that sort of thing."

Dammy complied, unimpeded.

"That's all right then," Xorialle said with relief. "A pity I don't have access here to the sophisticated equipment available at home, but these jury-rigs will have to do. Now, I'll just begin by teasing that reflex mechanism out into the open . . ."

A needle stabbed the sole of Montgomerie's foot at the same instant that a slim pointed rod jabbed at his face. He jerked his foot away and ducked sideways, throwing up both hands.

"Very nice," Xorialle called. "That gave me a splendid fix. We'll key everything to the reflexive response, you know—"

"I *don't* know," Dammy yelled. "You could have put my eyes out!"

"Hardly," Xorialle said mildly.

"At least you could have warned me."

"Dammy, please abandon this attitude of kindly protectiveness toward your own retrospective experience matrix. Anxieties are usefully directed only toward anticipated dangers, if at all."

"So what's the idea of jabbing ice picks at my eyes?"

"The basis of all advanced physical training is the redirecting of reflex. A karate expert, for example, learns to substitute for the normal defensive flinch a counter-offensive blow. Tap such an individual on the shoulder and very likely you'll be on the floor with a crushed trachea before he can stop himself."

"Yeah?"

"Speaking of karate," Xorialle continued . . .

Through the jungle of equipment, Dammy saw him punch a key. A bomb exploded immediately under him, hurling him into a wild gyration. His body and limbs threshed, quivered, spasmed; the equipment around him churned and writhed too rapidly for the eye to follow. He tried to yell, managed a croak. As suddenly as they had begun, the frantic contortions ceased.

"Help," he croaked. "Don't do it again. I'll talk."

"Now, that wasn't really so bad," Xorialle said absently, his eyes intent on the panel. "What say we take up prestidigitation next?"

"Is that anything like chewing a cud?" Montgomerie snarled.

"Your vocabulary is wider than you admit," Xorialle said. "We'll widen it still further this evening when you leaf through an unabridged dictionary of Terran languages I compiled the other day." He pressed a key, and clamps seized on Dammy's hands, twisted and wrung the fingers, madly flexed the palms and wrists, quivering violently all the while, simultaneously working his arms in frantic pumping motions, then abruptly ceased.

Dammy yanked his abused digits away, tucked them under his arms, where they tingled and throbbed as if stung all over by singularly mild-venomed bees.

"I feel like I've been squeezing an air hammer all day," he gasped. "What was that supposed to prove? I already told you I'd cooperate!"

"Dextrous hands are basic to many of the skills

that I'll be programming for you," Xorialle said calmly.

"How'm I going to have dextrous hands if you let this pile of junk beat 'em to a quivering pulp?" Montgomerie shouted.

"Nonsense, Dammy. I've merely imprinted certain action patterns in the manual area; the discomfort will soon pass. And you must confess the effort is far less in the aggregate than that which would have been required for hundreds of hours of practice at dealing an ace from the bottom of the deck or palming wristwatches, to say nothing of the tedium of an intensive program of isotonic exercises: you'll receive in a day benefits equivalent to some six hours daily of heavy workouts over a period of years—producing optimal hypertrophy of your skeletal musculature. You'll make Hoffman and Atlas appear frail by comparison."

"Sure, that's cool, Doc, but I don't want to look like a freak. Remember: W oc ps oc 1^3 x 1 = 1^4."

"Of course, of course."

"Just watch that l^3."

"Your physique will attract unalloyed admiration from all, I assure you. You'll want specially tailored clothing, of course, to accommodate your bulging quadriceps and so on—but that's a mere trifle. I suggest you dismiss your misgivings and simply enjoy the knowledge of your new skills."

Dammy looked at his hands, still festooned with weightless wires and rods and clamps.

"You mean . . . ?"

"Precisely."

"And before?"

"Karate, as I mentioned at the time."

"You're trying to tell me—I'm a black belt man now?"

"You have the physical tools of the discipline, yes. You have still to scan a text on the subject, giving you the applications for the various movements; but you'll find you can manage them flawlessly at the first attempt, just as a trained pianist can play a new concerto on sight."

"Yeah," Dammy said dubiously, "but how can I sword-fight, say, if I don't know one end of a sword from another?"

"In the case of a trained fencer, do you imagine that he consciously computes the path of a striking blade, extrapolates the future position of the point, decides on a response, and sets about tensing selected muscle groups in order to place his own blade in the desired relationship? Of course not. He merely reacts. Our task is to train your reactions."

"Uh-huh—but if you're from Mars like you say, what do you know about how a Chinaman makes bird's-nest soup or what it takes to ride a winner at Belmont?"

"My tape library includes recordings of mental patterns of selected experts in every category, covering both consciously and subliminally stored information relating to their specialties."

"I get it. You just waltzed up to Einstein and said, 'How's about it, pal? Want to sit under my hair drier while I pick your brains?' "

"Nothing so obvious, my boy. I have facilities for automatically seeking out what is needed and recording it selectively and at a distance. My collection now numbers over two hundred thousand separate human skill patterns."

"How long have you been spying on us, Doc?"

"Several centuries. It's a continuing process, of course. Even at this moment new data are being recorded. That's the clicking you hear."

Dammy flexed his fingers. "They don't feel any different," he said dubiously. "If I knew how to bottom-deal, I'd know it."

"Physical skills are imprinted at a level below the conscious," Xorialle pointed out. "If you were conscious of every move you made when walking, for example, you'd have room in your attention area for nothing else—and you'd probably fall down. The pianist looks at the music and his fingers play. In fact, if he's away from the instrument for awhile and becomes rusty, he can recover a tune he once knew by sitting at the piano and watching what his hands do. They'll strike the correct keys even if he's consciously forgotten them."

"I'll believe it when I try it and it works."

Xorialle casually opened a drawer, extracted a blue ball about the size of a pool ball, and tossed it at Dammy's face. He caught it easily and saw a second ball, bright red, coming toward him. Quickly he transferred the blue ball to his left hand, and the red ball slapped his right palm. Now a yellow ball was on the way. Xorialle was idly looking in the opposite direction as he flipped the balls toward Montgomerie, who swiftly tossed up the ball occupying his left hand and caught the ball shunted from his right, freeing it to catch the next ball. Orange, green, purple, black, white, gold, and silver. As each arrived it was integrated into the descending column of balls tossed up by Dammy's left hand—right, left, up, right . . .

"OK, so juggling's not so tough," he said, his

eyes intent on the flying balls. At that moment, Xorialle threw two at once, a brown and a pink. They joined the stream without visible disturbance. Then Dammy stiffened his right hand and held it at an angle so that the next arriving ball glanced off and rebounded past Xorialle's shoulder to land in the still open drawer, as did the rest, one by one.

"Hot stuff," Dammy said lazily. "Now I've got a racket I can always fall back on if times get tough."

"*Au contraire,* Damocles, you have several hundred marketable skills now, not all of the sideshow variety by any means. You could find employment in any research laboratory in the world as an expert in any of a number of specialties."

"That'll take some checking," Dammy said dubiously.

"There's no need to put it to test. I assure you matters are as I've described. Shall we continue?"

"That's cool," Dammy commented, "but if I'm trying to sell something, let's keep in mind $\frac{\Delta y}{\Delta x} = \frac{y}{x}$."

"Or, alternatively," Xorialle pointed out, "one might state the Law of Indifference as $\Delta y = \frac{y}{x} \Delta x$."

"You think I don't know first-year algebra, for crying into your homemade soup?" Dammy demanded. "Let's keep the discussion on a little higher plane, OK?"

"You react over-vigorously where no slight was intended, my boy. Now let us continue," Xorialle said mildly.

Before Dammy could object, another seizure gripped him.

"Skiing," Xorialle informed him blandly, and punched another button. "Freehand drawing,"

—*spasm*—"bird calls,"—*spasm*—"table tennis, jai alai, yoga, sword swallowing . . ."

"I feel," Dammy said three days later, "like I'd been run through one of those gadgets they use to tenderize cheap cuts of meat."

"You mustn't refer to yourself so disparagingly, my boy," Xorialle said cheerfully, stirring his martini with a swizzle stick. They were seated in deep leather chairs in the book-lined study. The thick, dark rugs, heavy drapes, the rough stone fireplace with its polished brass andirons lent a feeling of solid and familiar luxury.

Dammy sampled his drink. "I'm too tired to lift my glass," he groaned.

"Yes, it's been a busy time," Xorialle agreed. "And we have a busy afternoon ahead."

"No more today, Xorialle. I can't take it."

"You'll feel better after lunch and a nap. And the thought that you're now a master deep-sea diver, fly-fisherman, nuclear physicist, yodeler, stonemason, and window washer should console you."

"Funny—I'm still tired."

"I'll be most interested to see what we turn up in our next session," Xorialle said. "So far we've merely been bringing you abreast of current developments. Next I hope we'll break new ground."

"I don't think I like the sound of that."

"We'll merely be anticipating what humanity has in store for itself. No doubt today some individual somewhere is doing something for the first time ever. It may not be so spectacular as the first occasion on which a man lit a fire or added two and two, but it's still an advance. And some of these advances open the way to the exploration of whole new areas of unsuspected faculties. In a thousand years, ten thousand, a hundred thousand —who knows what you clever humans may be capable of, left to yourselves."

"Like what?"

"Do you know any nursery rhymes, Dammy?"

"What?"

" 'Mary Had a Little Lamb,' for example?"

"Sure. Its fleece was white as snow. So what?"

"Another?"

"Uh, 'Jack and Jill'?"

Xorialle placed a pad of paper and a pencil on the coffee table.

"I want you to recite *Mary Had a Little Lamb*—and, at the same time, write *Jack and Jill*."

"I can't do two things at once."

"Have you ever tried?"

"Well . . ."

"Try it, Dammy, just to satisfy yourself. I won't even watch." Xorialle rose and strolled across to the nearest bookcase. Dammy snorted faintly, but he picked up the pencil, paused for a moment, and mumbled, "Mary had a little lamb . . ."

"I'll be damned," he said a moment later. *Jack and Jill went up the hill* . . . was written in a scrawl across the paper, but a legible scrawl.

"So you see?" Xorialle turned to beam at him. "You can already do things you didn't think you could do. Now, I have work to do here. You have that nap and meet me in Studio Four in two hours."

"The method," Xorialle expounded two hours later when Dammy, again rested, was in position in the catalyzer, "is to explore your spontaneous bodily and mental reactions to various stimuli, trace the mechanisms employed, then extrapolate those mechanisms to their widest possible application. Suppose we begin with something simple: the so-called psychosomatic diseases—"

"Hold it right there; you're not giving me clap or cholera or something just to see what I do about it!"

"*Psychosomatic* diseases, Dammy. Imaginary ailments with real symptoms. Hypnotic trance, please, level one."

Dammy thought of arguing, but his eyelids were heavy; they closed.

"I'm going to touch your arm with the tip of a red-hot poker," Xorialle said, "but your arm is anesthetized; you'll feel no pain."

"Yes, but—" Dammy wanted to say; but it seemed too much trouble. He felt a light touch on his arm, heard a soft hiss.

"You may open your eyes."

Montgomerie blinked down at his arm. There was an ugly red patch at the point of contact. It swelled visibly, developing into an angry blister.

"Hmmm," Xorialle mused, studying his instruments. "A prompt vesicant effect, but no oxidation, of course."

"What did you burn me with?"

"Eh? Oh, that was my finger."

"A hot finger?"

"The heat was in your mind, my boy. You believed you had been touched by a hot poker, ergo you blistered. The symptoms of psychosomatic illness are quite genuine, as I said. Now, we'll merely make the machinery available to your conscious mind"—a sharp sensation flickered behind Dammy's eyes—"and now you'll find you can rise a blister whenever you like, at any point on your epidermis you choose."

"Swell—if you'll excuse the pun," Dammy said disparagingly. "Can I make 'em go away again?"

"Interesting point. Concentrate on remission."

"I would if I knew what it meant."

Xorialle sighed. "The dictionary was included in the material you scanned yesterday, as we both know."

Dammy concentrated. In two minutes the blister had faded, leaving a patch of colorless skin. Xorialle examined it.

"Some tissue damage due to the swelling; otherwise, back to normal. Now, some of the familiar symptoms most often imagined are headache, indigestion, hives, sinus infection, arthritis, heart murmur—"

"If you're planning on teaching me how to have an attack of *angina pectoris* for a party trick, skip it!"

"The mechanism, my boy, the mechanism. That's what we're interested in. If you can create a heart attack by imagining heart disease, you can also control your pulse rate, a most useful ability."

"Careful, Pop—play with my autonomic system too much, and I'll go into shock and fibrillation and a few other things, and they won't be psychosomatic."

"A little learning . . ." Xorialle sighed. "I'll take care, my boy; now just sit quietly and react as specified."

Dammy felt the feather-light touch of the questing tendril of alien thought in his mind. He had become accustomed to the constant presence of the alien intelligence among his thoughts, but now it seemed a gross invasion of more than mere privacy. He brushed it aside roughly. The next probe at the same point was firmer, carrying a note of insistence. This time Dammy deflected it just sufficiently to divert it from its intended target into an area of unresolved half-thought: impressions awaiting final filing. If Xorialle noticed, he gave no sign.

For the next hour Xorialle fired stimuli at Montgomerie, sometimes directing his response, at other times making note of his apparently spontaneous reactions. Dammy felt pangs, twitches, tics, twinges, in every part of his body in turn. He slumped with relief when his mentor signified that the session was at an end.

"Well, how do you feel, my boy? Intrigued in spite of yourself, resolved to cooperate to the fullest from now on?"

"Well," Dammy said, "you know how it is. I dunno. You know what I mean?"

"And stuff like that," Xorialle snorted. "Et cetera. And all that. Kind of. More or less. And so forth and so on. Ah, uh, oh. I mean. I guess. Damocles! Kindly spare me these vague, half-formed verbalizations and linguistic barbarisms! You know better!"

"Maybe," Dammy said indifferently.

"I'm disappointed in you, Damocles," Xorialle said. "In some ways you're not living up to my expectations."

"You're breaking my heart," Dammy said, and yawned.

"Your species appears to have one great weakness: mental laziness, in the face of which your full potential will never be realized."

"Sure, Doc. We all have our little flaws."

"Ummph. Well, we may as well continue. We'll check thought transmission next. Blank your mind, please, level two trance."

"I don't believe in that mind-reading stuff," Dammy said, but he closed his eyes. . . .

Gray mind-mist. Random images floating. Wonder if he can read me? Think about something else. Fast cars. Spaghetti dinners. The track on a nice day with a bill riding on the winner . . .

Something intruding—a new shape foreign to Dammy's mind, not the usual questing finger to which he had become accustomed. It moved, changed form, became words.

How do you hear me, Dammy?

"Hey!" Dammy said.

Don't speak! Think!

One, two, button your shoe. Abracadabra. How much wood can a woodchuck chuck. Ooly booly fooly drooly . . .

Damocles! Concentrate! Transmit 'I . . . hear . . . you.'

"Nuts, Doc, I—"

Silently!

Cautiously, avoiding contact with the alien shape perched impatiently in his mind, Dammy reached out tentatively with a phantom member. Awkwardly at first, then with increasing confidence, he felt his way out along the line of the current flow and skirted the looming, pulsating mind-glow that was Xorialle, tracing the leads of the electroencephalodyne back to their source. Space seemed to expand suddenly; he sensed complexity, the intricacy of elaborately commingled networks, felt the flow and pulse of energies, perceived the infinitely complex pattern that was the matrix underlying the mental field-effect.

He keyed his attention and total recall circuitry in the way that was now effortless, swiftly scanned the vast new data array before him, stored it in a remote corner of his mind, and keyed it to a retrieval mnemonic. Then he withdrew.

. . . *some effort to cooperate,* Xorialle was saying. *I'm sure* **you can** *do a great deal better, my boy! A time or two I felt that I almost sensed a vague psionic mumble from you, as if you were on the point of breaking through. . . . But no matter: you're not to be blamed for your genetic deficiencies. Still, if you tried harder . . .*

"Why should I?" Dammy said aloud. "It makes my eyeballs itch from behind."

Motivation, Xorialle thought in disgust. *That's what you lack, Damocles. You don't want to succeed!*

"When do we get to the part where I learn how to live forever?"

"Nothing simpler," Xorialle snapped. "It's merely a matter of cellular psychology combined with eidetics and controlled replication. Your preoccupation with the trivial does you no credit, my boy."

"Who'm I trying to impress?" Montgomerie asked innocently. "I didn't ask you to put me under a microscope—"

"Enough, enough," Xorialle cried. "Perhaps I'm getting old and tired; I've seen so many; the futility of it all sometimes overwhelms me." He appeared to pull himself together with an effort.

"But back to work, Damocles. Regulations require a complete profile; we may as well get on with it."

In the next hour, Xorialle attempted in vain to elicit from his instruments some fleeting indication of telekinetic powers lurking untapped in Montgomerie's brain. He probed his subject's potential capacities for awareness of objects and events at a distance, for predicting coming events, for communication with alternate planes of existence, for multidimensional conceptualization, controlled temporal displacement, matter transmission and duplication.

"Nothing," he said at last. "This is incredible! You're a psionic moron, Damocles—a psychic idiot, a nonobjective imbecile!"

"Oh, yeah?" Dammy retorted. "So's your old man!"

Xorialle sighed. "My apologies, Dammy. I'm disappointed. I had hoped—but no matter. One being's personal longings have no place in galactic policy. Let's call it quits for today. Tomorrow I have a few final points to clear up, and then . . ."

"Then what?"

"Then my job is finished," Xorialle said briskly. He managed a smile. "You must forgive my outburst. All indications had led me to expect great things from you; you're not to be blamed if they failed to materialize. Actually, all in all, you've done amazingly well. You've successfully absorbed an impressive mass of data, my lad, and all without disturbing your native temperament. In spite of being able to recite the literature of the world forward or backward, lecture knowingly on any subject known to Man, and outperform any champion athlete on the planet, you remain the simple, unspoiled youth you were when I plucked you from the gutter."

"Maybe so. But I'm kind of worried all this double-dome stuff will get in the way of living normal."

"*Normally*, Damocles."

"Suppose I said *normal-like?* Would you approve of that?"

"Hardly! A barbarism."

"Maybe. But *normally* is a corruption of *normal-like*, you know."

"Of course I know. I've watched the evolution of your illogical language with some interest."

"Tell me sometime about how the Romans pulled out of Britain," Dammy proposed.

"Somewhat before my assignment here. I know of it only by hearsay. But my predecessor had some fascinating anecdotes."

"How about the discovery of America?"

"I was a mere assistant technician at the time, attached to the Secondary Survey Mission."

"When was the Primary Mission here?"

"Some time ago, my boy, some time ago. You'd be surprised at the inaccuracy of the initial assessment."

"What about when Columbus discovered the United States in 1492?"

"You jape," Xorialle commented mildly. "Aside from that, even your own myopic researchers have determined that America was visited by Eurasians on many occasions prior to the formal discovery date."

"To be sure," Dammy agreed. "Israelites, Phoenicians, Romans, Vikings—the works."

"Those, and more. Polynesians, for example."

"Yeah, but Columbus was the first civilized explorer that found it on purpose."

"A number of your terms require rigorous definition, Dammy. But in essence, of course, you express your cultural bias toward members of your own ethnic group. Not unnatural, nor discreditable. Not even inaccurate. Merely limiting."

"So who *did* discover America? The Indians, I guess," Dammy answered his own query. "But what did they do with it? Nothing. I don't go for this 'noble red man' jazz. They're just *Homo sapiens*—some skunks, some right guys."

"Have you ever wondered why they were called 'red' men so universally by the first writers to encounter them? After all, their affinity to the people of eastern Asia is well established, and no one ever labeled a Chinese or an Eskimo red—aside from politics, of course."

"Beats me."

"Ah. Consider: the subgroup now known as the 'white' or Caucasian 'race' arose quite suddenly from the generalized aboriginal type in south-central Asia. These newcomers were possessed of a driving compulsion to excel—not merely to dominate, but to actually demonstrate their sense of innate superiority, a new concept in their world. One who sets out to prove that he is, indeed, a superior being frequently becomes an overachiever in the sense that, in searching for new ways to 'show off,' he investigates his psychosphere and comes upon great new avenues of exploration. Thus, the small seed group of pale-skinned men, surrounded by demonstrably different types who were instinctively inimical to the freaks among them and jeered accordingly, responded by breeding selectively for the very traits which the others despised, and indeed by claiming these features as badges of superiority. They then set out to prove their thesis. Soon they were established all across the temperate zone of the Eurasian continent, though they never crossed the Tethys Sea to Africa. In Europe, of course, they held their gains, while in Asia they gradually lost out. The Ainu and a few other isolated enclaves represent their remnant."

"What's that got to do with the Indians?"

"Oh, yes. I confess I lost the thread of my own thesis. The emigration across Beringia took place about thirty-one thousand years B.P., at which time the early pre-Caucasian types held sway in east Asia. Thus, the first arriving 'Indians' were white-skinned. They pressed on to the east across the Rockies and the Great Plains in search of the type of wooded terrain they preferred, which their fellows had found in Europe and North Africa, and which the immigrants of course discovered on the eastern seaboard. Deprived of the support of their home and society, they reverted to a more primitive mode of existence—though their long-houses and tools compare favorably with those used in Europe at that time. But excessive clothing disappeared. Remember that the Europeans of the Age of Discovery were not given to sunbathing. They lived their lives covered from throat to ankle. They knew nothing of sunburn. It was natural, then, that when they encountered sunburned men, they were struck by their bright pink coloration. Thus—'red man.' "

"I heard it was because they daubed red paint on their faces."

"A valiant theory, but untenable. Glance at a

contemporary portrait of Massasoit or Pocahontas. These were European faces. Of course, the continuing pressure of the Asiatic types who followed the first wave in time diluted and overwhelmed the east coast firstcomers. Though to this day the Mohawks, Algonquins, etc., exhibit a far less Oriental appearance than the Navahos, for example."

"So what?"

"Just chatting, my boy. I'm a bit nervous, I suppose, under the circumstances."

Dammy frowned. "What circumstances? Don't tell me you're starting to feel guilty about the way you snatched me."

"Not at all, dear boy. But, as I indicated, my work with you is essentially finished. . . ."

"So now you take me back to Chi and let me get back to my own business, right?"

Xorialle pursed his lips disapprovingly.

"Surely you see the impracticality of that, Damocles. I can't possibly release you among your own kind equipped as you are, knowing what you know."

Dammy wet his lips and swallowed. "What's that supposed to mean?" His voice cracked slightly on the words.

"Why—aside from the classified information in your possession—you'd be a virtual superman. I shudder to think of the impact you'd have on the orderly development of your world. It isn't ready for you, Damocles."

"Hey," Dammy said, "you're not planning on taking me back home with you to some place three hundred light-years away, I hope."

"Certainly not, my lad; set your mind at rest. Your remains will be interred right here on your home world."

"Remains?" Dammy croaked.

"You're a clever lad, Damocles," Xorialle said soothingly. "Surely you see that the only practical course is . . ."

"Disposal?" Dammy managed to get the word past his teeth.

"Disposal," Xorialle agreed.

"When?" Dammy whispered.

"Not until tomorrow, my boy. Now, what do you say to a nice dinner, a soothing alcoholic drink or two, a good night's sleep—and then . . . eternity."

"What do I say to that?" Dammy echoed. "I say it stinks! Let me out of here, you chiseler! You conned me into going along, and now all of a sudden you spring this 'disposal' stuff! Some pal. Some host. You won't get away with it. I still got a few friends, let alone a couple laws about kidnapping and murder. The snatch was a federal rap for openers, wise guy!"

"Good night, Dammy," Xorialle said quietly. "I'm sure we're both tired."

Comfortably ensconced in bed with his head propped on the fluffy pillows, Dammy eagerly turned his thoughts inward. All day he had waited for this moment. Now to examine more closely the inner wonders he had glimpsed last night . . .

He began hesitantly, mentally fingering the black bulk of the nullified 'control device,' then moving on more surely, tracing wide avenues that branched and narrowed, following the patterned logic he had absorbed from his first excited glimpse, fascinated by the wonders he found here, unused, in his own familiar brain. His eyes were open, his hands clasped behind his head. The ceiling above him was ornately decorated, he idly noticed for the first time. Intricate patterns evolved from a central boss. On an impulse to examine it more closely, he drifted lightly upward, casually flipping aside the light blanket. The nuclear bulge, he confirmed from close range, was a three-dimensional analog of the gravity gradient centered on a typical black hole. It was amazingly detailed, revealing the turbulence anomalies typical of the phenomenon. He dropped away, hovered a yard beneath the painted plaster. Idly he observed that he was drifting toward the west wall of the room at a rate of .073 meters per second, carried by the gentle circulation of air from the ventilating system. On impulse, he darted toward the register, stopped just short of ramming the wall.

"Got to be careful," he cautioned himself. Then, abruptly realizing that he was hanging unsupported four meters above the floor, he sank back to his bed and settled down, pulling the blanket to his chin.

"Teleportation. Wow!" he murmured. "Holy smokes, am I dreaming while I'm awake, or can I really . . . ?" He eased from under the blanket, rose a few inches, still supine, and made a quick circuit of the room. "Yep," he said softly, restraining his excitement with an effort. "Yep, I really CAN! And I'll bet . . ." He slipped back into bed, closed his eyes, and *extended* his awareness, feeling carefully along the corridor outside the room, down the lift shaft to the lower-level room where Xorialle, working briskly, was systematically smashing the delicate components within what Dammy recognized as an issue communication unit, tachonic, Mark IV, series 2769. Mildly puzzled, Dammy passed on, swiftly scanning through the remainder of the station, observing all details of every nook and cranny, noting a number of surprising items to be studied in more detail later. Then he *expanded* awareness, flashed across the winter seas, found the mainland, zeroed in on Chicago. Hovering, he felt out carefully for the familiar contours of his home quarter and dropped into closer range, focusing on the dark street where Jeannie lived. He found her house, dark and empty. Scanning outward from it, he found her—recognized her unique presence among all the others by a method he could not have described—and felt her shock, fear, desperation. What was wrong? He changed focus, saw that she sat in the rear seat of an automobile between two strange men. Another man—Chico himself—was at the wheel. The car moved fast along a dark street. Dammy lightly fingered the maze of fears and compulsions that was Chico's mind, impressed on it an action impulse. At once the man braked, steered the car to the curb, and switched off the ignition.

"Hey, what gives, punk?" the man on the girl's right snarled. He had a gun in his hand suddenly.

"Well, look, Frankie," Chico whined. "I got to thinking: why don't we just drop this caper right here? I mean, a snatch rap's no joke, and what do we—"

"Shut up," Frankie snapped. The other man in the back seat leaned across Jeannie. "Hey, Frank, maybe the creep's not too far off," he said softly. "We just walk off and leave this heap and the broad in it, we're in the clear. Otherwise—well, Big Jake don't care much if you and me go up, and like Chico said—"

"I heard what Chico said," Frankie cut in. "And we got our orders. I fer one ain't crossing no Jake Obtulicz. Take it easy, sister," he added to the girl as she pushed at the man who was leaning against her, leering down at her. "All Jake said was ride you around awhile, let you know it ain't healthy for no cheap broad to try to mix into the big man's business. That Montgomerie jerk—Chico seen him at your place. Now, that's unfinished business. Better get in line. Get moving, Chico," he barked in conclusion.

"No!" the girl retorted. "I absolutely won't help you ambush Dammy. Where is he?"

Right here, Jeannie, Dammy thought at her. *I'm OK. Don't worry about me. Do what they say.*

She uttered a sharp cry and sank back against the seat. "Dammy? . . . Where . . . what . . . ?"

It's OK, kid. Don't try to figure it out. A new trick I learned. Like a telephone—only better.

Frankie's hand reached out roughly to grab at the girl—and drew back abruptly. He scratched his head instead, eyeing Jeannie obliquely.

"You decided to get smart, sister?" he said, as if indifferent.

"Yes," she said. "I'll do what you say. But I hope he doesn't come."

"He'll come, OK, kid. Maybe you don't know what a nice build you really got on you." He chuckled softly.

Bye, Jeannie. See you soon, doll. Dammy, lying in his bed, was suddenly aware that he was utterly exhausted. He drew a deep breath and went to sleep.

Five

"Another helping of strawberries Bikini?" Xorialle asked genially at breakfast.

"Sure," Dammy said, yawning.

"I'm glad to see your appetite is good," the old gentleman said as he served himself. "But you seem listless. You mustn't let disposal upset you. After all, you'd have been dead days ago if I hadn't intervened. Just congratulate yourself on all the additional snacks and naps you've had."

"Somehow," Dammy said, "the thought doesn't console me."

"Hmmm," Xorialle muttered. "You seem tired. Possibly my idea of a last giddy round of pleasure last night was misplaced; I seem to have kept you up too late. I confess I've rather lost the knack of empathizing with lower life-forms."

"Speaking of lower life-forms," Dammy said casually, "what sort of report did you intend to file on me, on the human race?"

"Why, nothing out of the ordinary—an average emergent species with the usual modest capacities for routine functions."

"What sort of Concensus citizenship would that qualify us for?"

"Hmmm, Tenth Class, I should imagine—a perfectly respectable category largely made up of functionaries, bureaucrats, and routine executive types, with some small representation in the minor handicrafts." Xorialle pushed back his chair. "I suppose we may as well proceed directly to the business at hand. So if you're ready, my boy . . ."

Dammy remained seated. "I'm not ready," he said.

"Oh, surely you're not going to make a scene?" Xorialle said regretfully. "You should be able to accept the inevitable gracefully."

"I suppose it devolves upon the definition of the word 'inevitable,' " Dammy said in a level tone.

"Eh?" Xorialle cocked his head. "In light of your new awareness, it should be apparent to you that this is the only logical course."

Dammy nodded. "I've known since the first day."

Xorialle raised his eyebrows. "Then why the sudden show of reluctance?"

"This seems the appropriate time to inform you that there'll be a change of plan."

"Oh? And what change might that be?"

"I'm not going to be slaughtered today."

"See here, Damocles, putting it off until tomorrow would merely prolong the mental anguish you seem to be suffering—"

"I'm putting it off indefinitely."

Xorialle shook his head. "I'm afraid that won't be practical. My schedule requires the immediate closing down of the station and my prompt departure for home. Much as I'd like to indulge you—"

"I suggest you defer the destruction of the station."

"And why, may I ask—"

"You'll be needing it."

"I'll be needing . . . look here, Dammy," Xorialle said in exasperation, "this farce has gone far enough—"

"I agree. Accordingly, you'll drop the subject of killing me and proceed to complete my education."

Xorialle stared blankly at Dammy. Then he nodded. "I see; fear of dissolution has driven you mad. How very unfortunate, my boy; I'd hoped you could expire in a cheerful frame of mind, holding no grudges, savoring the new and final experience. As it is, I'm afraid I'll have to employ force. . . ."

Dammy felt the tentative touch of his mentor's mind-extrusion as it reached for his aorta. He brushed it aside, used it as a path for his own probe into the alien's brain.

This will hurt you more than it will me, he spoke silently. *Make no further effort to interfere with my metabolism.*

Xorialle, shocked momentarily into immobility, rallied and struck back. His psionic impulse lanced into Montgomerie's mental field—and struck an impermeable barrier. Dammy was aware of the alien mind reeling back, half-stunned by the impact.

"You were warned," he said coolly. "Shall we be going now?"

"You're making a great mistake," Xorialle said brokenly. "You can't do this! You'll bring down the wrath of the Galactic Concensus on you—"

"I don't suppose that will be any worse than a routine disposal," Dammy cut him off. "Do you intend to cooperate?" He gave a mild tweak to the alien's central sensory module. Xorialle yelped.

"What do you want of me?" he quavered.

"You haven't shown me all the lower levels of the station yet. Let's take a look."

"See here, Damocles," Xorialle said severely, "it's true you've managed to slip one over on me, to employ your own crude turn of phrase—"

"If you're employing one of my turns of phrase, obviously it's superfluous to so inform me. Quit stalling, Doc. Xzzppt!"

"Quite clever, my boy," the alien said thoughtfully. "You've managed to memorize a phrase of C-3. But are you aware of its meaning? Dear me, you've just threatened to give me a glimpse of my own intestines arranged as a wall decoration."

"Close," Dammy agreed. "I can understand now why you were a bit impatient with me at first. You know you're going to take orders in the end—so let's save time by omitting the ritual resistance. Szzxll!"

Xorialle shuddered delicately. "And all in the spirit of science, I suppose? . . ."

"Nope. Just for fun. Like this . . ." Damocles frowned momentarily, and Xorialle responded by emitting a sharp yelp and splitting down the center. The gray-glistening form inside the humanlike casing was quivering violently. Dammy frowned again; "Kquizlmp!" he buzzed. Xorialle closed up and straightened his tie.

"Don't do that again," Dammy said.

"You've shown me you've learned a trifle or two," Xorialle said. "Surely that should suffice. Now what? Tormenting me will profit you nothing. I don't suppose you've paused to consider your next step. You're still very much dependent on my good will, Dammy, but fortunately for you I'm a patient being. I harbor no grudge for the undignified events of the last few minutes. Sheer boyish exuberance, doubtless engendered by your sudden realization that yours are the secrets of bee-keeping, accounting, and modern dance! But don't imagine that my good nature can be imposed upon to the extent of treason to the Concensus. You speak casually of examining the lower levels. I say, Never!"

"What, never?" Damocles countered mildly. "Sxxzzpt."

"Never! Lower, or I should say 'emergent,' life-forms must not—but bother euphemisms! You'll not have a glimpse of the classified area, not that you'd understand if you did."

Montgomerie gave his tutor's main motor node a sharp jab, causing the dignified old gentleman to caper wildly.

"Why do you want to go poking about in the vaults?" he cried. "Nothing there concerns you! You won't understand it!"

I'll take that chance, Dammy transmitted mentally in Concensual Four, a highly sophisticated dialect reserved for formal occasions of the highest urgency.

"You cheated," Xorialle gasped. "You *did* absorb speedspeak!"

"True."

"You lied!"

"Quite correct."

"You dissembled!" the alien charged in dawning realization. "You pretended to be a dull-witted clod, and all the while you were looting the files, ransacking the library, leading me on!"

"Accurate, if not quite complete."

"But why? Why?"

"Curiosity."

"I misjudged you," Xorialle croaked. "Oh, I misjudged you badly. It wasn't only your intellect I underestimated. It was your capacity for duplicity and guile! My deepest probes into your psyche showed unmistakably that you share in your culture's avowed reverence for honesty, veracity, and straightforwardness!"

"And you planned to take advantage of my naïveté to use me like a tube of toothpaste and throw me away."

"Now, Dammy, that's far too harsh a view."

"You can add that item to your report," Dammy said. "We're not going to be rendered helpless by our virtues."

"Such cynicism!"

"Correct. And now that we've covered that, shall we go? You know where."

Reluctantly Xorialle accompanied Dammy down in the lift to the utility level. He paused there to attempt again to expostulate, but Dammy aimed a quick pulse at his pain center, which served to answer his arguments. The alien unlocked the security door—keyed to his distinctive alpha rhythm—and led the way down the narrow stairs.

"There are matters here, Damocles, which bear vitally on Concensual security, but which are of no possible value or even interest to you. Why challenge the vast counterintelligence apparatus of the Concensus at no profit to yourself? You're like a petty sneak-thief who idly rifles the local FBI office looking for petty cash."

"Zppttlt," Montgomerie replied. "You're still stalling, Doc. Let's start with Section Q-2786."

Xorialle turned to stare wildly at his former pupil. "Wha . . . how could you know anything of the Q category?"

"Never mind how. I do. Keep moving. No, to the right."

"Dammy! Listen, I beseech you. You've already accomplished something I would never have believed possible. You've forced me to permit you entry to Section M. Surely you see the wisdom of letting well enough alone? You're equipped now, as no man has ever been, to go forth among your own kind and achieve your every dream. I give you my assurance I'll return you safe and sound to Chicago—holding no grudge—and amend the record so as to dispel any suspicion back at Headquarters. It's a hard blow to my pride, but you pose no threat to the Concensus, so my conscience is clear. You return home, and so do I."

"What do you propose I do there?" Damocles inquired casually. "Open a bucket shop perhaps, and work my way up to a string of pawnbrokerages and gradually take over the rest of the action?"

"Perhaps," Xorialle replied vaguely. "The possibilities are endless. If you apply the philosophy of polo, for example, to the stock market—but naturally all this is obvious."

"Certainly it's obvious," Damocles said. "So why bother saying it? Incidentally, topological techniques would be far more applicable than polo strategy in playing the market."

"Well? Such cross-disciplinary approaches will

clearly make you a multibillionaire in a matter of weeks."

"Money is not the sole desirable goal," Dammy said. "It's a lubricant for the really satisfying activities, no more."

"You surprise me, Damocles."

" 'Do I contradict myself? Very well, then, I contradict myself. I am large, I contain multitudes.' Strange fellow, Whitman," Dammy mused.

"Let well enough alone," Xorialle pleaded.

" 'If a player is not well up on end games,' " Montgomerie quoted, " 'he may lose a game which could be won if he only knew how to end it.' "

"Hmmm. What has chess to do with the present contretemps?" Xorialle said testily. "Never mind. I see: You're conceiving this as a variation of the Philador Defense, following a Vienna Opening. Or . . ."

"Precisely—or," Dammy said. "Just give me a few minutes alone here, Doc. I promise not to break anything."

Xorialle glanced about at the walls covered by vaulted card-file drawers. "I don't know what you imagine you'll accomplish here, Dammy," he said in a resigned tone.

"That's right," Montgomerie said. "You don't."

Xorialle looked at him intently. "You have your victory, Dammy—all that you could ever have hoped for in your wildest dreams of glory. Now, of course, you'll want to return to the security of the nest. I urge you simply to accept your good fortune with glad cries and proceed on your way. With your knowledge of the law, medicine, psychology, et cetera, you need never know anxiety, want, or trouble of any kind. Take it and go!"

"You're in too big a hurry to get rid of me, Doc."

"See here, lad—I've been thinking," Xorialle blurted. "Why don't I simply make you a gift of the transmuter? Then you can run off a supply of doubloons, pieces of eight, double eagles, nickels and dimes, emeralds, rubies, and so on, as required."

"Nice try, Doc. But I'm not buying."

"I've warned you, Dammy. To meddle further here is to condemn yourself to certain death."

"Smarten up, Doc. We've already covered the disposal business. You can't cover your bet."

"Ah, Dammy, but if you presume too far, you'll feel the full weight of the wrath of the Concensus, which, I assure you, you'll not so easily neutralize as one lone representative far from home and getting on in years." The alien seemed to stifle a sob of self-pity. "I beseech you! Take all you want and go. But quickly!"

"I'm going," Dammy said. "But there are a few details to clear up before I settle down to a lifetime of pleasure. Through that door, lead on."

"NO! Absolutely not, Damocles! I draw the line—"

"Wrong. I'm drawing the lines now. Step lively, Doc."

The alien dithered for a moment, then opened the door and proceeded down a dim-lit passage, Dammy behind him.

After traversing well-stocked storage areas, they passed through chambers packed with softly humming apparatus on which colored indicator lights winked cheerfully.

"Better check the infraordinal retrieval syntach," Dammy commented. "It's running .0315 percent over optimal drain level."

"To be sure," Xorialle muttered. "I have my duties to see to, Dammy; kindly end this farcical affair."

"Before I go anywhere," Dammy pointed out, "I'll need transportation." He started across the room.

"Damocles, no!"

Ignoring Xorialle's expostulations, Dammy stopped before an unmarked door, noted its type, recalled the opening code, twisted the knob right, left, left, right, right, right, left, and stepped into the room beyond. It was a large chamber cut from the living stone, its walls and floor of glazed rock. Most of the space was occupied by an oblate spheroid, radially segmented, painted an eye-searing fluorescent tangerine. In a corner behind it Dammy saw a clear-plastic bubble with wheels and rotors that he recognized as the cycler in which he had been brought to Xorialle's hideaway.

"Well, now," Dammy breathed. He walked slowly around the twelve-foot-wide spheroid, discovering nothing to distinguish any one aspect from another, with the exception of an off-color disc half an inch in diameter in the center of one of the segments. He paused, then, introspectively considering the object before him, closed his eyes: *Three of spades*, he said silently. . . .

Vehicle: Intergalactic Mark XXXVIII, type 4, style zeeb; capacity: 25 solid nits; velocity (cruise): .876 lights; armament nil; retrieval code MB-5; classification FOOB; budget code: class 27 fleem, yunt; nonexpendable. Official Use Only. Penal schedule V38 applies. Maintenance Code 12-u.

"Yep," Dammy mused aloud, "I'm going to need first-class transport."

"In that case, lad, what about a custom-built Rolls Royce delivered to Chicago," Xorialle suggested hastily. "Hand-tooled leather interior, chinchilla rugs, built-in bar—or better yet, a small personal jet! Or possibly a hundred-meter diesel yacht, or even a nuclear-powered sub-surface craft which also does two hundred miles an hour on land and cruises nicely at an altitude of fifty miles—an all-purpose vehicle of remarkable versatility, though I wouldn't venture much beyond Luna in it—"

"You should have been a secondhand car salesman," Dammy said. "But I'm not buying while something better is available."

"Dammy! You wouldn't take my cycler! That's Concensual property."

"Sure. Like me."

"Now, Dammy, you're being unfair! True, I handled you incorrectly, but how could I have known?"

"Don't worry; I'll write you a glowing testimonial you can use at your court-martial."

"Dammy! I have it! Suppose I mock up a replica Bugatti *Royale*—you know nostalgia is all the rage these days—a perfect reproduction of the 1930 original (only six were built, you know, all for heads of state). A Bugatti *Royale*, I say, perfectly authentic in every detail, but with full class nine capability, of course. Think of the figure you'll cut cruising down State Street in that."

"You're still thinking of me as a Class Ten primitive whom you can distract with shiny baubles."

Xorialle shot Montgomerie a reproachful look. "An erroneous assessment, as I've freely confessed—but this is the first instance in my knowledge where a testee has deliberately falsified evaluation results to minimize his talents."

"How would recent developments modify the picture?"

"Class Two Special," Xorialle said promptly.

"Meaning?"

"Potential threat to the Galactic Concensus. Oh, not for many millennia," Xorialle added, "but Concensual policies look well to the future."

"Indicated action?"

Xorialle looked grave. "You made a serious error in apprising me of your deception, Damocles—of your true capacities. I could understand, and in a sense admire your gambit, if you had allowed my original impression to stand. In that case, your world would have been classified as a valuable though minor source of petty workers and administered accordingly. Of course, the error would have been discovered in time, but you'd have enjoyed an additional few centuries of carefree self-determination before the administrative routine got around to the matter of occupation and developmental controls. Of course, it would have meant your personally submitting to disposal, probably too great a sacrifice to expect of, er, a representative of so young a race."

"And now?"

"A Class Two Special rating calls for immediate drastic control measures, including population culling to eliminate undesirable traits such as aggression, imagination, initiative, and the like, followed by genetic segregation and redispersal in order to breed any specialized types that may be deemed desirable. Or, alternatively, out-of-hand planetary sterilization."

"Sounds swell," Dammy said offhandedly.

"As you see, there's nothing here of interest to you," Xorialle said quickly, edging toward a door. "I suggest we move along to the transmutation chamber. No doubt you'll want to take along a few hundred-weight of gold, as well as an adequate supply of corundum crystals, suitably colored and polished, and—"

"No trade goods, thanks," Dammy said. "I'm more interested in this thing. What do you call it, the Magic Pumpkin?"

"Oh, I see, a literary allusion. Most apt, my boy. But you'd find all this dull, deadly dull—"

"I need a range of at least a hundred parsecs in *that* direction," Dammy explained, pointing toward the wastebasket in the far corner of the room.

"But . . . that's . . . the vicinity of Deneb—and Concensual District Headquarters at Trisme."

"Right. And I want to get started right away."

"Damocles, no! You don't understand Concensual security arrangements! You'd be blasted to atoms the moment you intruded into Concensual-mandated space!"

"Not after you've given me the recognition codes and clearance procedures."

"But I can't, my boy! Those are matters of the highest conceivable classification! To divulge any part of such information calls for a mandatory death sentence, retroactive to birth!"

"Now who's acting out ritual objections?" Dammy said.

Xorialle wilted. "You're quite right," he said in a beaten voice. "Death is nothing; many's the time I've longed for it; but what would be the use of such a futile gesture? A Resurrection Team would simply reconstitute me and put me on trial for desertion. But pain is quite another story. I simply can't abide it. I'll give you the information you request." He sighed. "But, Damocles . . ." Xorialle looked candidly at his student. "You're making a mistake. I fail to imagine what possible errand you might conceive yourself to have Out There"—he flung out an arm in a gesture that encompassed the sky beyond the rock walls—"but I assure you that only swift extinction awaits the uninvited guest."

"OK. Consider me worried."

"To be sure, my boy, you've mastered nuclear physics, primitive aerospace engineering, brain surgery, and other quaint folk arts, but all, alas, without evoking the appearance of any of those serendipitous capabilities which I had hoped would emerge. You don't dream of the complexity of the society into which you so naively assume you'll insinuate yourself unnoticed. Tell me, for example, what would you do if confronted suddenly with a raptate of the Triarch of Gree in dastanic mode?"

"I'd accord it a rictus of category nine, with embellishment japt."

"A bit cheeky, I think," Xorialle commented absently. "What of this contretemps? A Glamorph of status eight is discommoded by a rynops while alighting from the transorbital vector at point 8076.31 b (minor). What is the indicated action?"

"An immediate recall of documentation from all vectoral mandales of phase three and wider."

"Of course—but I had in mind your personal on-the-scene response."

"A clace in the mode of Arfental would suffice, I should imagine," Dammy said nonchalantly. "Of more concern is the phase-resonance of the vectoral ambit, since I assume my planchet is at all times on valid mode."

"Damocles!" Xorialle broke in in agitation. "How—when—what could you possibly know of these matters? This is category ultimate material, available only to functionaries of the Zreeth impact, to be overted only under circumstances of class veeb!"

"If you'll refer to subparagraph 117B3972-H-144, with addenda, I think you'll find the situation covered," Dammy replied coolly.

"Ummm. But that means—"

"Exactly."

"Nonetheless, to invade Consensual space will be fatal."

"So I should just settle down and have fun while waiting to find out if we're to be used as docile workers or bred for dirty work, if not eliminated completely."

"Such are the realities of the Galactic Concensus, my boy. After all, as latecomers on the scene, you can hardly expect the Universe to conform to *your* wishes."

"Not good enough, I'm afraid," Dammy said. "That's why I have to do something."

"There's nothing you *can* do, lad," Xorialle said, wagging his head dolefully. "Take my advice and settle for overlordship of your own small planet."

"Strange," Montgomerie said. "A few weeks ago I would have jumped at it. Now it's not good enough. Not nearly good enough. What's the point in playing with toys while the floodwaters are rising all around me?"

"Ah, you begin to reap the first fruits of knowledge. The world is not so simple as it once was. The easy answers no longer apply." Xorialle sighed heavily, gave Dammy a shrewd look.

"You've won this hand," he said, "but I still have bargaining power. Even now I can help you—or I can hinder you."

"Watch it, Doc. You could get rubbed out for that kind of talk."

"Dammy, you wouldn't! You . . . couldn't? You were merely playing with me, pretending you'd steal the Mark XXXVIII."

"Somehow, Doc, I don't think I'd be happy if I went back to Chicago and resumed my career as a spotter for Little George."

"Damocles, the riches of your world are yours! With your knowledge, there's no limit to the height to which you can rise within your own society! You have the equivalent of postdoctoral degrees in every subject known to your encyclopedists! You've mastered every art and skill devised by your people since the invention of the hand axe! The world lies at your feet! You can return home and lord it over your former masters! Why throw it all away?"

"Oh, I dunno. Just hate to be pushed around by a Martian, maybe. Anyway, you'd better recode the VIM XXXVIII's entry lock," Dammy said. "Use this symbol." He projected a complex glyph in Concensual Twelve into his former tutor's consciousness. Xorialle gasped.

"Incredible," he said weakly. "I'll . . . I'll have to ask you to repeat; I didn't catch the fourth-order nuances."

"Never mind," Dammy said. "Clear the coding matrix and I'll key it myself."

"But—whatever for?" Xorialle protested. "You'll make it most inconvenient for me. You know nothing of the subtleties of its operation: you'd kill yourself if you attempted—"

"Forget it, Doc. You've got a backup on Special Level A, remember?"

"You know that, too? Then . . ."

"Sure, Doc."

"You know, my boy, in a way I almost wish you success. For many ages now, the status quo has been the highest aim of Concensual policy. But, I confess, from time to time I've entertained forbidden dreams, thoughts that intruded themselves unbidden into my mind—ideas of a fresh new wind blowing through the musty halls of Galactic civilization through doors opened by a young and vital race. When you 'failed' to measure up, I confess to disappointment, quickly suppressed, of course. As a Concensual official, what business have I in fostering rebellion? And now, though I know your effort is doomed, somehow . . . I feel an excitement stir. That's a sensation I've not experienced since King Xoser's reign. Perhaps, somehow—in some way—" Xorialle flopped his arms in a gesture of resignation. "But I'm raving. There's nothing you can do. You're going to your death, Damocles—a useless, unnoticed death—unless you'll change your mind and stay, to savor what you can of the carnal pleasures in the remaining twilight years of your race's youth and innocence."

"One thing puzzles me, Doc. You've got an alarm system here—an emergency backup, just in case. How come you haven't sent out a squeal to bring a couple carloads of Concensus cops in here to grab me?"

"Again, my boy, you touch a sensitive point. To be utterly candid, I dare not call for help for the simple reason that my work with you, far from being official routine, has been entirely at my own initiative, in contravention of the most basic imperatives of Concensual policy—a policy I thought shortsighted, but the dire utility of which has now been made woefully clear to me."

"Thanks for the tip," Dammy said. "But we're wasting time."

Six

The interior of the pumpkin-shaped vessel was a featureless, no-color, flattened womb, softly padded, unadorned.

"This is of course the neutral, rest-state decor," Xorialle pointed out. "You can, naturally, evoke whatever surroundings suit your fancy." He transmitted a series of mental symbols that Dammy automatically caught, interpreted, coded, and filed for use.

"These are my personal access glyphs," the alien explained. "You'll no doubt want to substitute your own."

"Naturally," Dammy said absently. Reviewing the contents of the manuals he had scanned was, he reflected, much like recalling some once-memorized but long-unrecalled poem. The words and paragraphs fed into his consciousness smoothly, as if supplied by some outside agency while he passively observed. It was all there, every detail of information needed to operate the fantastically complex machine that was the Concensual ship. It would not be necessary for him to ponder each move; the correct actions would come as automatically as the movement of a driver's foot toward the brake pedal when a traffic light turns red. Xorialle rattled on, supplying tips and bits of advice, which Dammy shunted to HOLD for later review.

"But I'm chattering like a nervous bridegroom," Xorialle said. "I surprise myself with the emotions generated by this development. But then, I imagine that these centuries of life among your people have had their influence on my mental and emotional processes."

"I should think you're isolated enough here that such influences would be minimal," Montgomerie commented.

"I've gone out among you many a time, Dammy. I've followed your progress. I studied the efforts of the first settlers of North America, as well as the life of the aborigines of Australia, prior to the first Western contact. The rapidity of your progress has always amazed me, but I never dreamed that one day one of your number would outfox me in my own den."

"Don't spread it too thick, Doc," Dammy said, giving his mentor a lopsided smile. "There were half a dozen ways you could have stopped me if you'd really wanted to. There still are."

"Nonsense," Xorialle snapped. "And now you'd best be on your way, if you really intend to go through with this mad scheme."

"Correct. Thanks for everything, Xorialle." Dammy held out his hand. With a show of reluctance, Xorialle took it.

"Good luck, my boy," he said softly, and turned away. "But don't quote me on that," he added over his shoulder.

Montgomerie stepped through the lock, which

valved shut behind him. He glanced around the amorphous room, then summoned up a series of mental symbols, directing them at sensitive points in the curving hull. There was a momentary sensation of pressure, of vast forces flowing impalpably around him. He was aware of a great hangar door opening, of the ship lifting swiftly, noiselessly, without discernible inertial effects—merely a vague internal disquiet. He smoothed away the discordance and settled himself on the curving, padded floor, listening to the whisper in his head as the instruments reported his rapidly changing position and velocity.

Time passed smoothly aboard the alien vessel. Tiring of the monotonous gray cell, Dammy used the sophisticated circuitry of the vessel to amplify his own new-learned mental techniques. He pictured a room he had once seen in a magazine. A hardwood floor with a rich rug appeared, vertical walls painted a soft blue-green, a white ceiling with a heavy cornice. Furniture of dull-shining mahogany came into existence, and a row of curtained windows beyond which was a pleasant view of sunny lawns and flowers, all highly convincing.

"Hey, not bad!" he exulted. "It works!"

He found the surroundings soothing for a time; then he grew bored, summoned up a rustic frontier cabin setting complete with crackling fireplace, plank table, rifle and powder horn over the door. That gave place to a dim-lit nightclub interior, for which he soon substituted a cheery neighborhood bar; then he lost interest.

Time passed. Dammy paid little attention to it, after making a few swift observations of relativistic effects. He spent his time lost in thought, scanning through the vast stores of data Xorialle's teaching devices had packed into his brain, marveling most at the incredible story of his race's long climb up from the tidal pools to the moon.

The moment came when it occurred to him to evoke human simulacra, though this taxed the capacities of the ship's sophisticated visualizer circuitry to the utmost. The conversation of his simulated companions was, he discovered, lacking in brilliance.

"Well, Dammy," said a stout, bleary-eyed old regular who seemed as much a part of the tavern scene as the end stool where he habitually perched, "where are we at now, hah?"

"We passed Pluto's orbit a few hours ago," Dammy replied.

"Oh, yeah? Well, I guess it's about time to switch over to, you know, trans-L drive, hah?"

"Another few hours."

"Yeah, on account of it gets like bollixed up with the local G-fields and all, hah?"

"Something like that."

"How do you know when to switch over, Dammy?"

"How does a Le Mans driver know how far to turn the wheel?"

"Yeah, I see watcha mean. Well, here's looking at you, boy."

There was a slim, dark girl who sometimes dropped in for a ladylike cocktail. Dammy had gently willed her to join him at his booth, but she demurely sat alone at a small table near the window.

He rose and went over. "Mind if I join you?"

"I suppose it's all right."

He sat. "You live around here?"

She looked almost at him; somehow, he could never quite meet the gaze of the habitués of his dream bar.

"That's a funny question."

"Is it?"

"You know I don't live anywhere. I'm not really alive. I'm just something you imagined." She shivered. "It's very strange. To be alive, and yet—to know that I'm not alive, that it's all a dream."

"I've felt that way myself. But I'm surprised *you* know. Anyway, I didn't exactly imagine you. I just set up the parameters and keyed the field to produce random consonant phenomena. I was kind of surprised when Woody first came in, and the others."

"What does it feel like to be . . . God? To have the power to create and destroy?"

"I don't think of it that way. I didn't intend—"

"You evoked human personalities, human minds. What did you expect? That we'd be hollow dummies, walking and talking, but not thinking or feeling?"

"I didn't actually think about it."

"Perhaps," the girl said thoughtfully, "I'm not really thinking. But if not, I'm doing something so similar that it has the same effect. I'm self-aware—whatever I am. I seem to me to be flesh and blood, but I know I'm not."

"I wish you wouldn't talk that way. It makes me uncomfortable. I wanted people here for company, not to make me feel like a monster."

"What you feel, Dammy, is your own business."

"Do you like being alive?"

"I don't know. I have nothing to compare it with."

"How is it you know you're not . . . real?"

"How do you know you *are*?"

Dammy laughed, not very humorously. "There's no end to this sort of conversation."

"Or to anything." She smiled past his left ear. She had a lovely smile. Dammy reflected that it was an instinctive animalistic grimace evolved from the primitive instinct to bare the teeth in threat; but it was still a lovely smile.

"Knowing things," he said, "doesn't change them."

"I thought it did."

"A heart specialist can understand every twinge of the cardiac arrest that kills him, but it kills him just the same."

"But not you, Dammy. You can control your heart. You'll never die of anything as silly as that. Or cancer or arterial disease. Your body will always be at its genetic optimum. And I suppose you can even change your genes if you want to; then maybe you'd grow taller, and your hair would be thick and blond, and your muscles would bulge more, and—"

"That's just it," Dammy said. "There's no point once you know you can do it."

"Then what is there?"

"I don't know," Dammy said. "I only acquired knowledge, not wisdom."

There was a small, rat-faced man in racetrack clothes who somehow reminded Montgomerie of Xorialle. He was, he suspected, an influence left behind by the ship's former owner.

"There's a lot riding on this caper, boy," the

little man said, and his necktie bobbled as he swallowed his drink, his bright, beady eyes on Dammy. "You're playing for high stakes, kid."

"I know."

"What you got to do, you got to do away with your preconceptions, like. Now, I guess you got some mental picture of striding into some big marble hall where the wise old Galactic Councillors are holding a board meeting and making a stirring appeal for the people of plucky little Earth. They'll admire the way you spit in their eye, and fix you up with whatever you want. But what do you want?"

"I want them to keep their hands and other grasping members off the Earth."

"What about the rest of the solar system? Mars and all?"

"That, too."

"And maybe you better throw in the next nearest couple stars, so's we have someplace to explore without running into their old beer cans."

"The whole volume of space," Dammy agreed.

"Maybe you better define volume. Anyway, why should they?"

"Nobody has the right to interfere with man."

The little man squinted his eyes, his gargoyle mouth curving crookedly.

"Have you—or maybe I ought to say 'we' just for atmosphere—got any right to interfere with the ants, say? Or to stick our noses into what the dolphins are up to?"

"We have intelligence," Dammy said. "That gives us certain rights."

"I'm not arguing with you, kid. But maybe those

boys out there got more intelligence than you do. What kind of right does that give 'em?"

"Not the right to kill us or enslave us."

"Have you got the right to kill rats?"

"I think so."

"Opinions, opinions."

"I want," Dammy said slowly, "the human race to have the opportunity to become whatever we have in us to become."

"Why?"

"Because it's our destiny. We have a tacit contract with the Universe that we can have all of it we can take for ourselves."

The little man snickered and turned away.

"I'm not saying it very well," Dammy said. "Maybe we don't have any rights. Maybe all we have is what the first life had that crawled out of the sea: an urge that we must follow, no matter what."

"Yeah—but that won't make the rest of the Galaxy go away, kid. They were building starships better than this one when the first cell replicated on Earth. They're there. They're what the Universe is like. It's a fact. They have their plans, too—plans that don't call for one cocky little tribe of hairless monkeys to stamp their feet too loud. They ain't going to go away just because you want room to swing your arms and yell."

"Then I'll have to make them give us room—whether they like it or not."

"How?"

"I don't know."

"Rots o' ruck, kid."

The time came to shift over to the radiation drive. Dammy could have written a complete and lucid text describing its theory, design, construction, and operation; but still he didn't understand it. Force fields were created which employed the substruct against which the velocity of light was measured, as a medium within which energies were channeled and directed. The material substance that was the vessel, being an alien intrusion into that substruct, was subjected to forces attempting to expel it. It fell along the lines of channeled energy. It crossed space in a time that was a fraction of that required for the propagation of electromagnetic radiation.

The little ship rushed outward—or, depending on one's frame of reference, it evolved serially along the time-space track. The nearer stars dropped astern. New suns waxed gigantic and dwindled again. From time to time Dammy caused the ship to become transparent to visible light, and then he rushed through space—or hung unmoving in the midst of immensity—naked to the Universe. A portion of his brain metered the passage of time in accordance with a dozen schemes of simultaneity; but consciously he had ceased to adhere to the now meaningless temporal structure. Events *were*: they existed in certain relationships to each other. And the events were those of the mind. There was nothing else.

Until the moment came when he encountered alien intelligence.

It was as though the boundless, lightless, crystalline sphere that was Montgomerie's extended awareness field had been suddenly pierced by a lance of energy. Succeeding walls of mental sensitivity crashed down; his mind-field shrank back in on itself, contracting to greater and greater density as he strove automatically to come to grips with the invading thrust, analyze it, counter it, halt it. . . . But it smashed remorselessly inward, striking down through Dammy's suddenly flimsy defenses to confront him baldly, a living, coruscating presence of tightly bound mindstuff, its surface awrithe with alienness, holding him fast, probing for information.

The interrogation, a remote segment of Dammy's mind noted dispassionately, required a fraction of a second—even after the inquiring intellect had discovered the necessity of "speaking" slowly and distinctly to its find.

What are you?

Damocles Montgomerie, human, Sol Three. Who are you?

Reference unknown. Authorization symbol?

None.

Status?

None—except that of a free intelligence.

A meaningless noise. Rationale for your presence in this sector?

I'm going to London to see the queen.

A meaningless noise of peculiar form (classify and investigate). Privilege citation?

None.

(A rapid interchange between the interrogating presence and another, too rapid for Dammy to follow.)

A use exists for you. Conform to standard mode———(A symbol followed.)

As the interrogation had proceeded, Dammy had cautiously traced the stranger's voice to its source. He met opacity, probed, found a point of entry, thrust carefully—

Stunning pain, a bombardment of silent noise that overloaded his receptors, sent him reeling backward, dazed and disoriented.

None of that! Behave like a civilized entity or you'll be dispatched at once. Conform to the specified transfer mode as ordered!

Dammy gathered his forces and struck suddenly at the probe at its point of contact. For an instant he was free, the pressure gone. He hurled coded impulses at the energy cores within the walls of his ship, felt wrenching pressures as it reacted, sensed time-space spinning past at a dizzying rate—

. . .*it and hold it!* The attacking mind's command blasted through his defenses. Forces clamped down on him, blanketing, smothering. He was aware of rapid shifts and realignments of stress patterns within his mind, of mental bulkheads slamming shut. Then blackness closed down, and all thought ceased.

Damocles Montgomerie awoke slowly, swimming up through multiple layers of awareness until he surfaced at a level of immediate pain, chill, discomfort. For a moment he clung to a fading recollection of the multiordinal infinitude through which he had just passed; then the complex abstraction broke, became fading wisps of thought-flavor, and was gone.

He lay on a smooth, slightly curving surface with the feel of a dense plastic. There were walls set at angles of no discernible significance, a high ceiling, dim light which emanated from nowhere.

Six feet from him, *something*—he sensed at once that it was a living creature—lay folded in an inert heap. A faint, uneven hissing came from it like steam escaping from a faulty valve. Its nubbly-textured hide quivered and twitched minutely. There was no identifiable head or tail. Dammy sniffed, detected an odor that reminded him of fresh-cut weeds.

He got to his feet. His body seemed abnormally heavy and clumsy. He ached all over; his head felt curiously hollow; there was a high-pitched, wavering singing in his ears. He felt bad, very bad. But nothing was broken. He was still alive, his heart beat, he breathed. These were the thoughts that ran through his mind compulsively, repetitively, as he explored the curious chamber in which he appeared to be sealed. Nowhere in the walls, floor, or ceiling did any sign of an exit appear. There were no plumbing facilities, no furnishings. Just himself and—whatever it was.

Dammy sat down and leaned against the wall. His mind felt strangely numb. It seemed as if a very long time had passed since last he had felt the necessity for thinking. He remembered certain events: Xorialle, the pumpkin ship, the girl with the sad, sweet smile . . .

The shattering assault of the alien mind.

After that, everything ended. Everything before seemed remote, academic, of no importance. Afterwards—there was only now.

"I'm Dammy Montgomerie," he said aloud. His voice sounded muffled, as if he were speaking into a blanket. He thought of repeating the statement, but it was too much trouble. There was no point in it. It was easier to wait.

"No, dammit!" he said aloud, and struggled to his feet again. It was hard work. He felt as though his interior were packed with wet towels, limp and impossibly heavy. Braced against the slanted wall, he probed at the material of which the surrounding surfaces were composed. His mental impulses bounced back as from a mirror. He searched for a seam in the unbroken shell around him, found none. He was as isolated as if buried at the heart of a dead planet.

The creature lying folded on the floor groaned—a long sighing groan. It stirred, quivered, unfolded.

Gossamer, iridescent wings, in every color of the spectrum, erected themselves like a gaudy tent, fanning out, spreading ten, fifteen feet wide, uncovering a small body, partially Chinese-lacquered in gold and scarlet and blue, partly clothed in black velvet. A face of the complexity of a bee's looked at him.

"You're a noisy fellow, aren't you?" a light, clear voice said. Dammy heard the voice, understood the words. At the same time, he realized that on another level of interpretation, the creature had uttered only a single mellow tone, like a plucked cello string. He recognized it as a dialect of Concensual Nine.

"Sorry," Dammy muttered. He felt the clumsiness of his mouth as it shaped the word. He tried again, heard himself make a sharp, harsh sound.

The creature quivered its wings. "Not so loud, please!" Dammy stared at its face, trying to identify which of the jewellike beads of color or glints of facets were its eyes. For some reason it seemed important to look into his cellmate's eyes when he spoke to it.

"Sorry," Dammy said again, making an effort to speak softly. The winged creature crouched as if struck.

"I have a suggestion, if you don't mind: whisper."

"What is this place?" Dammy buzzed, realizing suddenly that he, too, was now speaking Concensual Nine.

"Better. Much better. I'm grateful. So many entities one encounters have no conception of a polyordinal value system. I predict that we'll get on very well. Where do you come from?"

"Earth." Dammy amplified his reply with a swift imagery of the solar system, then of the entire galactic sector, showing Sol in relation to Centaurus, Barnard's Star, Wolf 359, the Luyten, Sirius, and Ross systems, Epsilon Eridani, the Cygni, and the Procyons.

"Oh. Umm. Out there, eh? Rather remote area. Wasn't aware of Concensual penetration so far out. Still, one is always recording new data, eh?" This was the way Dammy interpreted the other's sounds, even as he listened to the short burst of speedtalk. The underlying assumptions and biases of the alien creature seemed to express themselves in familiar, Terrestrial terms—an act of interpretation on his own part, Dammy realized, a bucolicism, on a par with an American GI's pronunciation of foreign words as their nearest English homophones: donkey shine, three beans.

"You didn't answer my question," Dammy said.

"Yes. Well, rather awkward, you know, attempting to match a spatial identity concept to a dynamic locus. But I suppose one could state that we're occupying a vital support transfer encapsule. Is that the sort of abstraction you had in mind?"

"Where are we going?"

"No data."

"You're a prisoner?"

"I see you have a need to verbalize concepts before they can be fully integrated into your status gestalt. Curious. But to each kind its foibles, I always say. Yes, I'm a prisoner."

"Who's our captor?"

"A minor trade-route official, I gather, a Vocile Napt. My contact with him was brief and unpleasant. It seems he's in need of cheap labor to replace certain attritional losses."

"What kind of labor?"

"The usual, I suppose. Assimilation, collation, abstraction, discretion and value judgment specialists—all that sort of thing. There's a chronic shortage of computational capacity in the suboriginal category, as you doubtless know—"

"I don't know anything. What's your name?"

"Eh?"

Dammy strove to communicate the concept of an identifying ego symbol.

"Curious," the winged alien commented. "Most curious. I am myself—who else? And yet, I see that your need to attach a non-unique nomenclature to a unique phenomenon is nonetheless real for being redundant. That being the case you may think of me as . . . Floss."

"All right, Floss—how do we escape?"

Dammy received a momentary impression of mental blankness, followed by an amorphous emotional impact of surprising weight.

"Escape?" Floss echoed, with overtones that Dammy interpreted as shocked wonder. "To remove ourselves by an act of volition from the compulsions imposed by Concensual authority? An astonishing concept. Can you be serious?"

"I've got things to do and places to go," Dammy said. "I don't have time to be anybody's slave."

"You have a directness of thought which shatters my composure," Floss said. "Have you no reverence for tradition, no respect for the establishment, no fear of consequences?"

"Not a bit," Dammy said.

"Amazing," Floss commented. "Utterly impossible, wildly impractical, and foredoomed to failure—but still amazing and curiously exciting."

"How much do you know about this place?" Dammy asked. "How do they feed us? How did we get inside? What's outside? How many guards? How long before we reach wherever we're headed? Any weapons aboard? What—"

"Wait, wait!" Floss cried, and folded his gossamer wings to half-mast. "One concept at a time. Escape. Escape! Is it really possible to consider such a thing?"

"Anything's possible," Dammy said. "The rest is details."

Precisely four hours, nineteen minutes, and twelve seconds, Earth rest time, after he had first awakened in the alien prison-ship—so Dammy's internal clock advised him—an iris dilated at one side of the featureless chamber, and two four-inch aluminum-surfaced spheres popped through. Dammy lashed out at once with a tracer impulse, had time to sense the existence of a network of autonomic circuitry linking a multitude of life-support, navigation, and drive devices to a central power core before the opening scythed shut, cutting off his probe as if by a guillotine.

"Nothing can be that impervious," Dammy said, driving a shaped impulse at the wall with all the force at his command. It was much like aiming a two-cell flashlight at a brick wall.

"You're an astonishing creature," Floss said. "The shielding isn't impervious, of course; as you rightly sense, that's a physical nonsense-concept. But it *is* a highly effective reflector. Still," the alien added, "I see you gleaned a certain amount of information before the sphincter closed. Rather clever, that. You *do* move quickly, if in surprising ways. Tell me more about this home world of yours, Damocles. How long has it been since it was incorporated into the Concensus?"

"It wasn't. And it never will be."

Floss found this statement as remarkable as all of Montgomerie's other comments. He asked questions. Dammy answered tersely.

"Unheard of," the alien said when he had exhausted his inventory of questions. "A wild world, a free-growing organism outside the structure of Concensual organization! Fascinating!"

"As I understand it," Dammy said, "the Galaxy is full of independent worlds—until your Concensus finds them. Then it gobbles them up, stamps the inhabitants into molds, throws away what won't fit, and goes on—like a steamroller building a road through an ant colony."

"The discovery of a new species—particularly a mentational species—is not a common occurrence. And of course the standard procedure is to classify any such organisms and put them to use, thus avoiding waste. The idea of a primitive life-form actually taking the initiative, seizing a ship from a Concensual officer, and, wonder of wonders, penetrating Concensual space—well, you'll have to excuse me, old fellow; it's almost too much to assimilate."

"Doesn't anybody fight back?"

"It isn't actually a question of fighting back, in the sense that I perceive you mean. There's no choice offered in the matter—any more than a domestic beast such as I see in your memory has any voice in its fate. It finds itself alive, it does what comes naturally to it, it's harvested one day without warning or comprehension. So it is with the simple peoples gathered in by the long arm of the Concensus."

"Does that program satisfy you?"

"You have a knack for the disconcerting question. Satisfy? What constitutes satisfaction? Had I infinite control over matter, time, and energy, I'd rearrange affairs in a different configuration, of course. But what configuration? Let us suppose I were troubled with hunger; I'd satisfy that hunger with nourishment—or would I? Why not dispense with the need for food instead? If I lacked companions, the approval of my fellows, why then—I'd surround myself with friends and render them properly appreciative of my achievements. But if I have the power to engender appreciation, why bother with the achievements?"

"That's too complicated for me," Dammy said. "Let's stick to what we know: that we're locked in and we want to get out. That's a straightforward question with a specific answer."

"To get out, you say. My thoughts leap forward to speculations as to a subsequent course of action. What role awaits an escaped chattel? What niche can such a one hope to carve in the temporal flux?"

"One thing at a time, Floss. How much do you know about this capsule we're sealed inside of?"

"Little enough. Oh, I've used similar ones, of course, but never queried their structure."

"What's it made of?"

"Again, your questions imply a most baroque bias, a structure of underlying assumptions of outlandish character. Still, I'll attempt to enter into your spirit. 'Made of,' you say? Not 'of what energy pattern is it composed!' *Made*. What can be made can be unmade, you imply. And—perhaps you're right, Dammy! Why not? Why not?"

"The spheres that popped through the iris," Dammy tried another tack, "what are they?"

"Nourishment. I wondered why you hadn't consumed yours."

Dammy looked across the room at the two globes lying where they had fallen. One, he saw, had lost its pearly iridescence.

"I thought I had the Universe by the tail," he said sadly, "because I knew the native handicrafts and had even learned some of the things a mind is for. And I wind up in a dog pound where the keepers assume the strays can teleport food from a sealed container into their stomachs." Dammy paused. "Which raises the question: why didn't they teleport the stuff through the wall? Why a physical opening?"

"You're making a false assumption, Dammy," Floss said. "There are no keepers. This vehicle is unmanned."

"Now we're getting somewhere. No crew, eh?

Just you and me and the walls. What's outside this room? Can we stay alive there?"

"Vacuum, radiations of various sorts, the stressed-space field itself—"

"What steers the ship? Where is it going? What kind of power?"

"The capsule was coded for some destination; naturally, it goes there—"

"How?"

"Why, how could it do otherwise?"

"We have a communications problem," Dammy said. "You assume too much, accept too much, don't ask enough questions. Maybe I'm making the opposite mistake. Stop and think: it could do otherwise if it malfunctioned."

"Malfunction," Floss mused. "Another of your outre concepts: a device designed for a function, failing to perform that function, performing instead, perhaps, some other function—or no function at all. Wonderful! Dammy, already you've injected more novelty into my existence than I had ever hoped to encounter in a full span!"

"You have a lot of fun with my questions," Dammy pointed out, "but you don't answer them."

"Glancing into your mind for a parallel," Floss said, "it's as though someone asked you, 'What if the sky fell? How far is up? Why don't hens give birth to kittens?' Still, your point is well taken. I'll not attempt to fit your queries into the pattern of my own rationale; I'll merely supply data, and you'll compute from them in your own way—and we'll see what results! Now, as to your queries . . ."

Floss explained that the capsule was a shaped energy vessel; that it drew its power from the tensions existing in the fabric of space-time; that its destination had been encoded in its structure at the instant of its formulation, as much a part of it as was a living cell's genetic makeup.

"Mutations happen." Dammy extended the analogy. "Genes can be modified."

"But there must be access to the plasm. Here, there is none."

"When will the valve open for another feeding?"

Floss communicated an elapsed-time concept. Dammy interpreted it as twenty-one hours and four minutes.

"What about waste disposal?"

This was another question which amazed and appalled the alien. Among known mentational races, it appeared, such biological inefficiency as a requirement for casting off unusable molecules did not exist.

"Good," Dammy said. "That makes the thing that locked me up not quite so infallible. He, she, or it overlooked something. Maybe it overlooked something else. Are there any other openings in the walls?"

"The valve, as you call it, is not precisely an opening," Floss corrected. "It represents a moebian discontinuity in the force field—"

"Skip that part," Dammy said, "unless it's going to help us take over the ship. I'll go on thinking of it as an opening."

"There is no other opening."

"I saw some of the circuitry," Dammy said. "Take a look."

The touch of Floss's mind in his was as light as the brushing of a faint breeze over grass. By comparison, Dammy realized, his own mental probes were clumsy, insensitive blunderings. Swiftly Floss scanned the patterns in Dammy's mind, indicated a major nexus point.

"A random pulse initiated here should have a highly disruptive effect on the function gestalt," he said.

"What if it isn't a random pulse? Why not redesign the gestalt and feed in a shaped pulse that will reroute the capsule?"

"I suppose it might be possible, assuming we can strike quickly enough, with precisely the correct vector—"

"We can design the pulse we want. And if the two of us link together, push at the same time—"

"Dammy, I'm beginning to think it might work! A slight reorientation *here* . . . a modification of the pressure pattern *there* . . ." With deft touches, Floss pointed out to Dammy the sequence-form of the necessary recoding pulse.

"If we should succeed in assuming control," he said, "it will be a purely symbolic act, of course. The Authority will not permit us to exist as random factors in the Concensual status quo. But the satisfaction of the act is in itself sufficient reward."

"I disagree," Dammy said. "But we can take that up after we're free. What destination are we changing to?"

"We'll merely disrupt programming and set the capsule on a random course; does it matter?"

"Where do you come from, Floss?"

"A minor world of a minor sun, just as you, Dammy. Why?"

"Why not go there?"

"Go back again to Almione?" Dammy caught a hint of the wave of alien nostalgia that the thought of his birthplace had evoked in Floss: kaleidoscopic images of green sunlight on broad yellow meadows, forests of mauve trees casting magenta shadows, great wings spread in ivory moonlight.

"To go back again," Floss repeated. "To see once more the place of my beginnings, perhaps to reweave the fabric of my destiny in a new, more fulfilling pattern—but this is fantasy, of course. The Galaxy is so immeasurably vast, Dammy—"

"We can try," Montgomerie said.

"I can well believe that you come from a race of wild beings, unbroken to civilization," Floss said. "You voice conceptualizations that cut across half a star age of convention. A part of my mind bids me recoil in horror from the chaos implicit in your existence; but another part that chafes under the restraints of life reaches out to link with you in your folly."

"Good," Dammy said. "Let's make our preparations."

Time, Dammy had noticed, passed at unpredictable rates when his mind was fully occupied. Computations that would have required hours in the days prior to his training could now be accomplished in less than a second, but when he turned all his attention to a complex problem, immersing himself fully in its ramifications, tracing out multiple lines of hypothesis to their conclusions and integrating the latter, postulating new parameters and recomputing, hours would spin by unnoticed.

When he and Floss had completed their analysis of Dammy's split-second glimpse of the capsule's circuitry and had prepared their counterstroke, Dammy came back to full awareness of his surroundings to realize that he was exhausted, and that only two hours remained before they would make their attempt. He stretched out on the resilient floor and blanked his mind for sleep.

What are you doing? Floss's query came into his thoughts.

Sleeping. Probably a primitive habit you've done away with long ago. But you shouldn't have. You don't know what you're missing.

Wait! I feel you slipping away—

I'll be back. Have to sleep now. Tired . . .

"Dammy!" The alien's shout shocked Montgomerie awake. He sat up. Floss hovered in the air, his wings spread, quivering. Light from an obscure source shimmered in their gossamer texture.

"Why do you have wings?" Dammy inquired. "They look fragile. I have a much easier method." He assumed the levitational mode and rose easily from the floor. At first, great effort was required to hold himself aloft; but it quickly became easier. He darted around the strangely shaped room, swooping past Floss, who recoiled, fluttering his wings. The walls, Dammy saw, were more complex than he had thought. Instead of being sealed at the corners, they overlapped like the flies of a stage setting, with a space between them wide enough to slip through. Dammy eased past, found himself in a crooked passage. Fresh air blew in his face. He pressed on, Floss's cries growing fainter behind him, following the many twists and turns of the route. Now light glowed ahead. He brushed past a hanging curtain of vari-colored beads and was on a high terrace, colonnaded, open to the sky. Below, a lagoon of unearthly beauty was clothed in morning mist. Far away, islands seemed to drift, half-seen in the fog. Tinkling music that seemed to speak of enchanted forests came from some invisible source. Under Dammy's feet (he was walking now) marble slabs were cool with the slumbrous chill of the deep earth.

He went forward to the balustrade that edged the terrace. A cliff fell away sheer below him to a curve of white surf coiling at the edge of the blue sea. Far above, small white clouds rode like fragments of an unattainable landscape, islands in a magic sea. The vast, clean emptiness beckoned to him. He stepped to the curving, carved stone parapet, leaned forward, waiting for the pressure of the wind to bear him up. . . .

He was falling, heavy as stone, paralyzed, not able to move, not even able to scream. He struggled, managed a groaning cry. . . .

Floss was beside him, his folded wings streaming in the wind. He reached out with arms as thin as twigs, as wiry as vines, gripped Dammy, spreading his vanes against the rush of air. He saw the glory-colored pinions stiffen, their delicate membranes stretched taut, and felt his headlong fall slow. Then the ribs buckled, the tapestry shredded, whipped in tatters in the wind. Enfolded in the polychrome shroud, they fell together in darkness, amid a great rushing that rose to a roaring like the cataract of Niagara. . . .

With a supreme effort, Montgomerie ripped free of the entangling fabric, twisted to assume the flying mode—face down, arms and legs outflung, head back—and willed himself to soar. . . .

Impact shocked him wide awake. He was lying face down, his back arched, his arms and legs straining outward. For an instant he waited for the overwhelming pain of destruction to sweep over him. Then he became aware of Floss's voice calling his name. He croaked a reply, rolled over, sat up.

"Dammy! What happened! How . . . ?"

"Must have had a nightmare," Montgomerie said. Slowly, the dream visions faded.

"I was with you," Floss said, and there was awe in his voice. "You took me with you into a stranger land than any I've ever known. It was a world you made with your mind, and though I knew that, it bound me as straitly as any fourth-order continuum."

"Sorry," Dammy said. "It was involuntary, you know."

"You frighten me, Dammy," Floss said. "I looked into your mind and saw deeps beyond all measure; and you roamed there, making and destroying Universes like an insane God."

"It was just a dream."

"I should turn away," Floss said. "Something there is in you untrammelled and without discipline, energetic with a wild force the Universe has never known. You frighten me—and at the same time you give me hope."

"Don't go mystical on me," Dammy said. "I'm not responsible for my subconscious."

"Therein lies the danger, and also the hope. In the beginning I regarded you with a tolerant amusement, as a novelty, an outré diversion to lend a note of variety to my foreordained fate. Now—I am amused no longer. Great forces stir in Cosmos, Dammy, and through your strange mind I caught a glimpse of them. I am repelled and attracted. I see how small my grasp of multiordinal reality truly is, what a petty role intelligence has played. When you spoke first of escape, I quaked at the enormity of challenging the petty order of things. Now I see that the Concensus is but the scum on the pond of reality and that a great ocean lies beyond. I fear it—but I would sail it, even to my doom."

"Good," Dammy said. "Get ready; the valve will open in four seconds."

He triggered the mental signal that readied the prearranged attack pattern, felt Floss's delicate yet powerful mind-field merge with his. There was a shifting of forces, a turning and reorientation of energies in the immaterial shell that surrounded them. An aperture appeared; together they struck, expanded to occupy and become identical with the web of force lines that were the essential stuff of their prison; with swift, precise thrusts they realigned the tension matrix, reset coordinates, redirected the contrapuntal flows of field energy. Reality shifted frames of reference; there was a sliding of intangible interlocking planes, a meshing of great non-material gears. Somehow, things were . . . different. Floss fluttered his wings excitedly.

"You seem to have found a plane of permeability among the energy laminars," he said in a tone of astonishment. "Pause a moment that I may assimilate the concept on a mathematical basis."

"Slow down," Dammy said. "You're getting ahead of me. You noticed that I unlocked the stress interlocks, which would, of course, bring the endocosm into identity with the exocosm, and—what are we waiting for? Let's get out of here!"

"Will you accompany me to Almione? Or had I

best not attempt . . . ? It is indeed a fragile and tentative conceptualization you have offered, strange being."

"If it works, use it," Dammy suggested.

"Dammy! Again you astound me. Your logic has the stark beauty of Pamindore's theorem. But let us begin."

"Oke," Dammy muttered aloud, feeling the curious writhing of his face and tongue even as the syllable roared and reverberated in the enclosing space. Floss cringed, drew his wings close. Dammy shut his eyes, felt out for firm footing ahead. The clinging muck dragged at his extended leg, but he forced it, probed—and found purchase. With a great effort, aided by a firm grip on a thorny hanging vine, he lunged again, gained the respite of a spongy hummock, and looked back for his companion. In the gloom that was perpetual even here at the edge of the great miasmic swamp, the frail figure was barely visible.

"You OK?" Dammy called softly.

"Dammy, I'm stuck," the whisper came back, vibrant with suppressed panic. Dammy used his sheath knife to hack away the entangling vines, labored to the alien's side. The hot, wet air seemed as heavy as a soaked blanket.

"Come on," he urged. "It's not so far." He grasped the lean hand of Floss and led him across to the firm patch he had found. Nearby, something uttered a harsh squawk and made splashing sounds. Floss clung to Dammy.

"Perhaps we'd better go back," he quavered.

"Just as far around the Universe one way as another," Dammy pointed out, and pushed ahead. Subjective hours passed. Dammy was suddenly aware of fatigue and the pain of innumerable thorn scratches. Poor Floss struggled gamely behind him, uttering faint cries from time to time. Repeatedly Dammy had gone back to extricate the fragile creature from mud or vines or a barrier of interlocking twigs. At last firm ground appeared ahead, dimly visible by the light of a small, pale moon—a rising slope of featureless gray. Dammy managed the last few yards and fell face down, exhausted. It was odd, he reflected, how similar was the surface on which he lay to the floor of the prison capsule. He opened his eyes, saw the familiar walls around him. Floss crouched nearby, grooming his wings.

"What—" Dammy started. "How—after all those hours—or days?" Floss seemed unconcerned.

"Incredibly," Floss remarked a moment later, "I believe we have achieved success."

Life in the prison cell was in no way different after the takeover. There was no sensation of movement, no indication of passing time other than the periodic delivery of nourishment and the concomitant expulsion of wastes—a matter with which Montgomerie had dealt by the simple expedient of telekinesis into the emptied capsules, which he then expelled into the surrounding medium, the nature of which remained indefinable in terms of any of the sciences of Earth.

The passage to the original destination might have required several months of subjective time; Floss, being unsure of the intended course, could be no more specific than this. The trip to Almione, he estimated, might take a month, in Earthly terms. The concepts of velocity and distance being relative, no closer calculation could be made in the absence of more data. And there was a possibility, he reminded Dammy, that they would never arrive at all.

"In fact," he pointed out "we may be standing perfectly still, relativistically speaking. Our meddling may have negated both the spatial and temporal transposition torsions, leaving us stranded high and dry on a null space-time stratum, where we may remain forever."

Dammy proposed that efforts be made to extend some external awareness mode to assess the nature of the capsule's relationship to the exocosm, but Floss dissuaded him.

"An attempt to monitor our progress might interfere with the phenomenon we seek to examine. Let's let well enough alone."

Dammy was forced to agree. Time passed slowly. He spent large segments of it exploring the new data in his mind, but eventually this palled. It was much like reciting the multiplication tables, he found. The data were there when needed; but the need for the findings of petty disciplines evolved in the narrow context of a geocentric science were, it was obvious now, sharply limited.

"I can tie flies, draw wire, tan leather, and repair electronic microscopes," he mused. "Employment wanted. Reasonable rates. All work guaranteed."

"Don't grieve that your folkways are of limited utility," Floss consoled him. "We all learn that lesson. You'll find the basic mentational patterns adaptable to new situations. Be patient, Dammy. When we reach Almione you'll doubtless find diversion in mastering the technique of life among an alien, though I trust not inimical, species."

Dammy tried, with limited success, to summon up the phantom figures who had kept company aboard Xorialle's versatile vessel. He was able to induce hypnogogic hallucinations of remarkable verisimilitude, but they seemed no more real to him than so many line drawings. He soon became bored with the pastime. Floss lapsed for long periods into a comatose state from which he could be roused easily enough by a telepathic call; but the alien seemed little interested in conversation for the sake of conversation. He resisted Montgomerie's suggestion that he tell him of his homeland.

"Soon you will see it, Dammy. Or, alternatively, you will not see it. In the latter case, knowledge of it will be of no value; in the former, your own personal impressions will be more accurate than my verbalizations and depictions."

So time passed. Dammy slept—keeping a segment of his mind aloof from uncontrolled dreaming, and waking in time to prevent another disturbing incident. He scanned literature, bringing buried material into the forefront of consciousness, evaluating it, assimilating it into his world picture. He practiced his newfound abilities, performing acrobatics, doing mental computations, reviewing his own past in detail. The latter experiment depressed him, and he discontinued it.

"Even without what happened to me," he told Floss, "I could have done so much more than I ever attempted. The story of my life is a running account of lost opportunities, missed chances, unmet challenges. There wasn't a day in my life that I couldn't have experienced something worthwhile. But I didn't. Any progress I made was random, with almost every instinct warring against a feeble flicker of curiosity. I had ambitions—but they were ambitions within a framework of the trivial. My idea of self-improvement was buying—or stealing—a fancier car. My conception of progress was wearing flashier clothes. I had youth, health, a good brain; there was nothing I couldn't have done within the scope of the world as I knew it. I could have been king of the planet, a great scientist, an artist, anything—or all of them."

"And a fish could swim out of the net—if he understood the nature of the net and of his own capabilities. But he doesn't. And neither did you. Now you know more. Not much, true—but more. Perhaps someday you'll begin to learn some truly valuable relationships. It is a thing to hope for."

"I thought I was a genius," Dammy said. "When I took over from Xorialle and made my decision to come out here, I thought the Universe was my oyster."

"You'll learn, Dammy," Floss said, and sank back into his dreamless sleep.

And on the ninety-fourth day after their attempt, the capsule, without warning, winked out of existence, leaving Dammy and Floss sprawled on soft violet grass beside a scarlet lake.

Seven

"It's not like I thought it would be," Dammy said. "Nothing's the way I thought it would be." He and Floss rested on a spongy dais of living moss under a canopy of broad blue leaves beside a curiously shaped structure which the alien assured his guest was a dwelling belonging to whomever chose to use it.

"And at home, in your own place, Dammy, did everything accord with your expectations?"

"No, but that was different."

"That, too, eh?"

"I can breathe the air," Dammy said tonelessly. "The gravity is about right, maybe six and a half percent light. There's no lethal radiation from the star, no instantly deadly diseases. I don't believe in coincidences like that."

"No coincidence," Floss assured him. "Our captors could not have placed us together in an environment inimical to either of us; thus my world is safe for you. As for diseases, I see the concept in your mind, but no such parasitic life-form has existed in a civilized world for ages uncounted."

"I thought a spaceship would be a destroyer-sized rocket," Dammy went on, "all metal walls and cramped quarters and stale air and machinery. I thought space travel would be like sitting in a cockpit looking out at the stars. I thought arriving somewhere would be noisy and bumpy and exciting and dangerous, and that there'd be a welcoming committee or a lynch mob waiting, and forms to fill out and shots to take and lots of solemn discussions with the authorities about my passport and who I am and what I want, and that you'd have to argue eloquently to keep me out of jail or save me from being deported, and that then I'd set to work to organize a Save the Earth Committee, and—"

"Dammy, I perceive that you amuse yourself with these ramblings. You expected none of those things. You have a curious habit of first conceptualizing stereotypes and then formally verbalizing them, as if to reassure yourself of the structure of reality. Surely this is unnecessary in the light of present circumstances. Come," Floss proposed more jovially, "let me show you my little hideaway."

He led the way along a nearly concealed path between feathery fern beds of a pale lavender that contrasted nicely with the violet grass. A faint perfume like distant lemon blossoms floated in the still air. Rounding a turn of the path that skirted a finger of purple-black woods, Dammy caught his first glimpse of the house. It was a bubblelike structure with pale translucent walls, perched on spidery supports not unlike Floss's thin legs. The alien paused to wave a hand.

"Behold my nest," he said genially. "Lacking genius in art or science, or a vital post in the societal mechanism, I've lavished such skills and enthusiasms as I possess on creating this small island of peace and order. It has been my challenge to make it perfect—within a limited interpretation of the concept of perfection, of course. Each entity, living or inert, has its own potential; to fulfill that potential is to perfect the entity. Thus, I have labored to create here the optimum blending of beauty with utility. Each function, color, texture, and form is balanced against the others to create a harmony to rival that of the natural setting. Here nothing was left to chance, every atom was planned; there has been no compromise with ease or cheapness; all is of the finest and is maintained flawlessly. There is no corner where error and filth accumulate. It is, in truth, within its modest scope, the material expression of my perception of the harmony of the Universe, the collation of all that I hold precious. . . . But I discourse at length. Come, let us experience the degree to which I have succeeded."

He led the way along the curving path through beds of vivid blossoms, across a small but immaculate spread of purple-red grass, and halted suddenly. Dammy saw foot-wide divots of turf incongruously gouged at random across the lawn. Four small bushes bearing white blossoms lay uprooted.

"I chose this spot far from our great centers of society for the purity and the stillness of the air."

Floss paused to twitch a complex earlike appendage which Dammy recognized as an olfactory organ. Simultaneously Dammy noticed that a faint whiff of a garbagy stink had intruded in the gardenia scent of flowers. Somewhere a shrill squeaking sounded, a piglike squeal. Floss turned slowly to face the source of the sound. At that moment, a dull detonation *thump*!ed, and beyond the bubble house, a tall tree shivered violently and slowly toppled out of sight, while fragments fountained to rain back, a few splinters of tangerine-colored wood dropping harmlessly beside the two observers. Floss turned to Dammy, his beelike features moving rapidly in unreadable expressions.

"All is not well, Dammy. Best you hurry to secure a place of concealment—there." He pointed toward the depths of the purple-black woods.

"What's happening?" Dammy asked, peering toward the house. Now quick-moving figures in mole gray coveralls had moved into view, tall, forward-leading, scuttling on short legs. Floss uttered a cry.

"Teest!" he exclaimed. "That which I greatly feared has come upon me!"

"They're a long way outside Teest territory," Dammy remarked. "I take it there's no legal reason for them to be here?"

"None," Floss moaned. "My great heo tree, sacrificed already, and—" He pointed. Now Dammy could see the intruders moving busily inside the bubble house.

"What do they want?" Dammy asked.

"Want?" Floss echoed. "What they want is what they have obtained: destruction. There can be no negotiation with them; they live but to destroy. Woe that they have sought me out!"

"What will you do?" Dammy demanded.

"I must save what I can," Floss said, moving forward. "Then one day I can begin again." He hurried toward the house along a path of colored tiles, past a small fountain that threw a sparkling jet fifty feet upward to fall back in jewellike drops into a shallow pool where pale blossoms floated. Beside it fragments of a delicate sculpture lay scattered on the sward. At once there was a stir among the strange, shoulderless, thick-torsoed Teest now gathering in a group before the house. Three moved forward as if to intercept Floss, who made no effort to avoid them.

Dammy reached out with his thoughts, felt the mindless life emanations of the vegetation, a faint murmur against which Floss's anxious half-thoughts mumbled vaguely. A cluster of hard-edged alien cerebration fields buzzed, oblivious of observation. Dammy stepped off the grassy path, leaned against the bole of a tree in deep shadow, closed his eyes, and *probed*. . . . He encountered the textures of barbed wire, torn metal, and splintered glass; total and utter hostility radiated from the cluster of vandals a hundred yards distant. He caught impressions of acrophobia, impatience, urgency, frustration—gnawing emotions which raged unslaked. Then more precise thoughts came into focus.

. . . *before the return of the Great One!*

. . . *strange, helpless life-thing. It is blind.*

. . . *something I mislike . . . there! did'st feel it?*

NO! The negation slammed at Dammy like a bomb burst. The ragged textures closed, pinching off sharply. Dammy felt gingerly along the 'edge' of the blanked-off alien mind-glow, found an interstice, poked inside . . . and was adrift in churning sound, raging light that tossed him until he broke through into an aching void at the center. In the abrupt stillness, he examined the interior of the linked mindfields that had resisted him for a moment. The Teest, he observed, were simple creatures who, incomplete in themselves, strove for completion in group thinking, a technique which increased their effective intelligence into the human range; thereafter they sought fulfillment in unreasoning destruction; thus they lived, in conflict with the Universe, their great hungers unappeased.

Then, suddenly, Dammy was aware of the close presence of sharp, encircling thought-forms. He withdrew from deep contact, leaving behind a confusing impression of sudden dissolution as camouflage. At once the sharpness of the alien thought probes relaxed into an aimless bluntness that fumbled uselessly for a moment before wandering away—to flash in an instant back to the central hunger. Dammy opened his eyes to see two of the ferretlike creatures strolling, apparently at ease, across the grass a few yards distant. Beyond them, Floss struggled feebly in the grip of three Teest, one of whom was plucking at the gossamer wing membranes of the harmless creature. As Dammy was about to step forward, a crowd of Teest surged into view around the curve of the shrubbery masking the foundation of the house. Dammy drew back and watched as others came singly or in twos or threes to join the conclave, until fifty-one were grouped facing one of their number, distinguished by a black cap and a glinting sidearm. The squeaking Dammy had heard before resumed. The speaker waved his short arms. His listeners stirred, then froze at a shrill yap. Floss, unattended, slumped against a small tree near the house. Dammy touched his mind.

Fly, he urged. *Use those wings!* Floss failed to

stir. Only a listless negation came from him. Dammy felt carefully for the harsh mind-shape of the leader.

. . . *zeal!* he read. And . . . *feed full, but first*—As the alien thoughts cut off, the orator whirled to stare toward Dammy's casual concealment. Then he resumed.

. . . *some treachery. Quick, now! Let all be accomplished ere last zat! Remember you toil under the eye of the First!*

The audience dispersed at once, some to stream back out of sight to the other side of the house, others fanning out across the lawn where they paused, apparently at random, to gouge turves. One went to the fountain, tossed an armload of black muck-backed sods into the clear water, which at once turned to murky foam. This vandalism completed, the creature moved on to a flowering shrub covered with pale pink, fleshy blossoms. On impulse, Dammy reached out to the plant and to his astonishment encountered cerebration of almost faunal intensity. Clearly the forb was aware of danger and felt anxiety. At that moment, the mind-stab of the Teest slashed savagely at the plant, which was now visibly trembling. The alien animal paused and uttered a prolonged squeal at which the plant blushed a deep pink. Its weak mindfield flickered in terror. The Teest drew a curved blade from its broad belt and stepped in. Dammy took two steps behind the creature and caught its upraised arm, jerking it back violently. The Teest squealed savagely and whirled, its underslung jaw snapping at Dammy's arm, missing by ten point nine seven centimeters, Dammy noted, as he dislocated his opponent's limb—carefully, so as to occasion no permanent damage; then he thrust the bestial being away. It staggered back, squealing in a whining way, holding its injured arm close. Then it turned and scuttled away.

Two nearby Teest, alerted by the frantic squeals, abandoned their attempts to fire the dry grass at the woods' edge and closed in on Dammy from either side. He stood fast and extended awareness to finger the incomplete minds of the furious creatures. He observed as they attempted to link up like badly fitting fragments of a jigsaw puzzle, only to abandon the attempt and concentrate their effective thoughts on the destruction of the hate object before them. Dammy thrust sharply at one of the baffled part-minds, felt it shatter into its equally ill-matched components along sutures of frangibility representing the incremental evolutionary history of its kind. The creature faltered, dropped to all fours, ambled aimlessly away. The other nearby drew his knife and closed in warily. Dammy countered him almost absently with an unfocused mind-blow. He, too, reverted to a quadrupedal gait and headed for the shelter of the woods to Dammy's right.

There was a stir among the Teest near the house. The fire set earlier was crackling among dry brush stalks and low boughs immediately downwind from the building. Floss was again in custody, walking awkwardly with his arms and wings bound to his sides by turns of heavy rope. Objects were raining from the house, tossed down by the busy workers inside. Floss skirted a heap of shattered furnishings, seemingly indifferent to the vandalism proceeding all about him. His captors jerked at him roughly, steering their compliant captive into the deep shadow east of the looted house.

Dammy reached out to contact his friend's mind but encountered difficulty; the background clatter of the Teest clump-minds intruded. There were now four groups of twelve, he noted, none functioning so smoothly as had the five original Ten-Teest sets. After the loss of the two segment-minds Dammy had broken, the two thus bereaved groups had at once disbanded, their members insinuating themselves into still intact groups which had received them readily enough, but had not yet fully integrated them. Accordingly, the remaining functional Teest worked now with less purpose and organization. The black-capped Great One, normally in absolute authority over his minions, was having difficulty now in eliciting discipline, or even simple attention. The individual Teest now milled aimlessly in a loose group, falling back on the ancient pre-mind instincts to form a pack for food searches and physical defense. Long-buried reproductive impulses surfaced, and pairs casually coupled, heedless of their master's fury. Here and there an individual, his role in a group-mind confused, reverted to the quadrupedal gait. Suddenly fire gouted near the main group; the confused creatures shrank back, leaving two of their number kicking on the scorched grass. Dammy felt their shattered mind-fields wink out. The Great One advanced on his cowed followers, a curiously ornate weapon in his hands, assumed a stance between the corpses, and menaced his remaining minions with the fire gun. They quickly retreated, pressing close together. One who delayed was instantly flamed. At last Dammy felt a trembling contact with Floss, who, again abandoned by his captors, crouched, his mind radiating apprehension. Dammy attempted to rally him. *Come on, Floss, now's the time to take to the tall timber. Run that way!*

The only response was a sense of vast amazement.

But—they wouldn't like that! his feeble thought came through. *I must wait for my instructions.*

Why? Dammy demanded. *Wouldn't you rather be free to do as you like? Maybe to throw these spoilers out of here?*

Floss registered unfocused astonishment. *Dammy! Again you offer me eerie vistas of a curiously distorted Universe view! How do you evolve these outré notions with such seeming ease?*

Easy, Dammy replied. *First, I consider what I'd really like to do, and then I figure out how to do it.*

Breathtaking, Floss thought. *Just like that! Have you not considered the terrible revenge these rascals will take, to say nothing of the provisions of the Raptate Code?*

Nope, not for a second. Let's get busy. I need to take the big shot's rubber-band gun away from him before the whole landscape's covered with his pals.

But that might be dangerous, Floss countered.

Uh-uh, Dammy responded. *I won't hurt him.*

Floss persisted. *I meant to you, but I see you jape even now.*

Dammy faded back into the cover of the woods and began making his way silently toward the house. He sensed a quadrupedal alien watching him ahead, felt the simple creature's mindless lust to kill the not-Teest—or, more precisely, to dismember it. The Teest moved parallel to Dammy's course, closing in. Dammy watched it more in curiosity than apprehension. It was dimly visible at intervals as it stole as noiselessly as himself through the dense underbrush. Suddenly it darted up the trunk of a major tree, ran out along a branch which overhung Dammy's route, and flattened itself against the foot-thick bough. Its mind-field was a kaleidoscope of dimly realized images of violence, the tearing of flesh under fang and talon, juice trickling down the parched throat, and at last, physical satiety.

Dammy studied the Teest mind.

The Teest were born to their groupings, he perceived, each set being usually made up entirely of siblings. Offspring were, at birth, assimilated in the overmind of the mother of the litter. The development of the immature Teest mind was thus formed by the already existing group to which it was added. Only rarely did a newborn Teest mind possess sufficient self-sufficiency to strike out on its own to form a new combination or to join one more congenial than its native one. The Great One, Dammy realized, was such an exceptional individual. Now, alone and free for the first time since it had come into existence in the final days of fetal development, the mind of the Teest found itself faced with the necessity for solitary decision making, a problem which effectively paralyzed its will.

Interested, Dammy examined the stunted mind-field that lay exposed before him. Here was a creature which, from birth, had been denied any concept of self and had existed uncertain, incomplete, an aching void at the center of its world concept. It was in an attempt to soothe that vast, gnawing insecurity that it turned so readily to the violent tearing down of the hostile, rejecting environment. In place of a latent creativity, the maimed creature sought to assuage by destruction its egoless craving for—something. Functionally the difference was a slight one, Dammy saw at once; with a touch *here*, a thrust *there*, a quick readjustment of flowing energies, he reoriented the Teest mind on a new basis. For a moment, in shock, the construct flickered, wavering; then it realigned itself, struck a new balance, and reached an equilibrium it had never known before. Gone was the turbulence at its core.

Hell, I'm not here to solve these boys' problems, Dammy reproached himself. *I'll leave the exopsychiatry to a classification team. Right now, I'd better do something smart.*

Above Dammy, the Teest stretched its limbs aimlessly on the bough, forgetful of the impulse that had brought it there. It looked down past Dammy, rasped its yellow claws against the purple bark; then it yawned, leaped down casually, and strolled away. Reaching the edge of the lawn, it resumed bipedal posture, went briskly to the nearest upturned clod of turf, and with deft forepaws replaced it. From there it went on to the next and then the next. In five minutes it had effaced all signs of vandalism from a quarter of the small lawn; then it went on, pausing now and again to pick up a scattered sculpture fragment or bit of paper or cloth blown from the scene of destruction, tucking each into a capacious leather pouch slung at its side.

Suddenly aware of fatigue, Dammy cleared the twigs from a patch of grassy ground under a spreading shrub and stretched out. He slept immediately.

* * *

The prodding was insistent. Lying at ease in the big bed, Dammy wished the damned fool would go away. He groaned.

Dammy! The frantic mind-voice of Floss penetrated his lethargy. *Where are you? Are you—?*

I'm swell, Dammy responded curtly. *Lemme sleep. I'm beat.*

Floss persisted. *For a long time, I couldn't feel that fantastic I-field of yours! Sleeping again, were you? I thought they'd destroyed you.*

Dammy sat up groggily, blinked, unrefreshed by his nap, and stared, uncomprehending for a moment, at the shadowy foliage around him. Then he rose and scanned about him for any near presence. Floss was still one hundred and four point-three-one meters distant, beside the house, he noted. No Teest were near, but he could hear the voice of the Great One delivering a spirited harangue. The sun had set. Floodlights had been brought up to set off the area around the house in a blue-white glare. Soon the speech ended, and the audience, now seemingly disciplined once more, dispersed purposefully. Bearing lanterns, small parties of half a dozen entered the surrounding woods at widely separated points, then dispersed.

Dammy followed their actions visually for a few moments, then turned away—to see lights approaching him from behind. Quickly he scaled a rough-barked tree and took up a position shielded by overhanging foliage. He rested there, listening to the sounds of breaking brush and squealing voices. One searcher came close, paused at the spot where Dammy had slept. It applied a canelike instrument to the spot, then followed Dammy's trail to the point whence he had watched the organization of the search. After a moment the Teest fingered a device at its belt, then came directly to the base of the tree where Dammy had taken refuge. Now others were converging on the spot. Silently, Dammy eased to his feet on the broad branch, walked along it as it narrowed to a point whence he could step to a bough of an adjacent tree. As he did so, a ghostly memory of numberless hours of practice under the big top flitted through his thoughts. He remembered a graceful redheaded girl who had taught him the secret of the "Triple." Poor Molly . . . what had become of her after Blatman had folded the show? . . .

Shaking off these idle reflections, he directed his attention to the problem at hand: Directly ahead, his progress was impeded by a curtain of intertwining vines armed with six-inch spikes, red-tipped, and, he knew, virulent. Below, visible through the foliage that screened him, a considerable crowd of Teest had gathered. Their pale green, torch-tipped poles clustered now into a continuous eerie glow. As Dammy turned to survey possible alternate routes, vacant Teest faces turned up, pink snouts glistening, red eyes searching the gloom above for their quarry. He froze, but it was clear that if they had not actually seen him, they sensed in some way that he was there. One of them casually raised his firefly-colored 'torch,' and violence blasted chips from the bough near Dammy's feet. There were two more quick blasts. The last seared his left shin, charring the leatherlike shipsuit he had provided for himself while still aboard the Magic Pumpkin. He suppressed the pain and bleeding at once, but the injured leg was weakened; he felt it folding under him.

By a quick leap he managed to gain the nearby branch, avoiding the poisoned spikes close beside him; but it was a clumsy leap, and he clung precariously as the Teest below squealed and trampled brush. Light-beams and blast-beams poked at the foliage around him, splintering and scorching, but none struck him. At length they moved away, concentrating on a point some twenty feet behind him. It was apparent that they assumed that the sound of his leap had signaled a retreat to the safety of the main trunk he had originally climbed. After twenty-eight minutes and forty-one point three seconds, Dammy was sure they had lost the trail. Silently, trembling with weakness, he moved down, reached the ground behind the tree unnoticed, eased himself under the concealment of a spreading, juniperlike shrub, and concentrated on emergency healing of the scorched skin and muscle tissues of his lower leg.

Over two hours later, after three close brushes with luckily less-than-alert Teest skirmishers beating the brush beyond the main body, he came in view of the Teest vessel. It was, he noted, a standard Bogan number three (utility) hull, a simple and, for its kind, highly efficient plus-L ship. Only half a dozen feeble docking lights outlined its prow against the blackness of the clearing it had burned out in landing. But the sentry, probably to alleviate his apprehension, had set up a small glare node which conveniently illuminated the entry valve. Dammy settled down to wait, noting in the superficial mentation of the lone Teest occupant an intention to emerge and check visually on the situation. Then he decided to arm the antipersonnel field first. Dammy knew all about the Bogan A-P field: he would have to wait.

He got as comfortable as he could lying on damp twigs and sharp stones and rose straight up, not forgetting to dodge the branch just above him—only somehow he was still feeling those sharp-cornered pebbles digging into his chest and thighs. Funny—he tried again, and almost didn't succeed, but then he felt the weight ease off, and he was levitating—just barely. *Brother, I've got to have food in a hurry,* he thought. *I'm operating on my stage three vital reserve right now. If I don't get fed fast, I'll be one of those 'heart-failure' cases they find without a mark on them.* The food looted from the house was aboard the Teest vessel. None of the vegetation around him was assimilable by his Terrestrial stomach, he knew. He made an effort that made him see little bright lights, rose a few inches higher, and eased in toward the silent spaceship, sensing the periphery of the trigger field of the A-P device ahead. *Got to get above it,* he thought laboriously.

He noted barely in time that the light breeze was drifting him dangerously close and caught at a near-at-hand branch. It snapped, causing him to execute a slow roll during which one foot penetrated the alarm envelope. At once a sharp *whuff!* sounded, and he felt the stinging impact of a hail of tiny crystals which crashed through the foliage like thrown sand. They were, Dammy knew, a wide-spectrum nerve paralyzant. He had, perhaps, one-third of a second in which to act before he fell, dead, to the forest floor fifty feet below. His solution was to impel himself toward the nearest tree with the last ergs of his strength, and the ancient primate instincts saved him. Unconscious, his hands caught and clung as his feet groped, found purchase. He started down, and then instinctive reflex failed and he fell.

Waking up this time is worse, Dammy was aware of himself thinking painfully. *Compound fracture of the left tibia, he noted, and never mind the details. Still, I'm not dead. Odd.* He checked inwardly and found that his cells, responding to subliminal conditioning of which he had not been aware, had rejected the poison, encapsulated the pellets, and thrust them to the surface, which no doubt accounted for the grainy feeling and the itch. The educated cells had also, he noted with surprise, broken down the invading material and extracted energy-yielding molecules before rejecting the detritus.

Now for a real meal, Dammy thought. He reached out with somewhat renewed vigor, scanned the interior of the Teest vessel, located the loot, including the contents of Floss's larder, selected a container of a bland legume puree, and teleported its contents into his upper intestine. This chore accomplished, he turned to the problem of the shattered limb.

Dammy. The mind mind-touch of Floss came then. *I see you didn't remain in the west thicket as I advised you. No matter. It's plain we'll not meet again. But before our destruction, do tell me: why? Why did you attack the Teest? I've puzzled over it for hours now, and I'm still at a loss. They offered you no threat; it wasn't your property that was being destroyed. You could have evaded them un-*

til they were finished and then emerged to continue your singular existence. But no; you stayed—and not content to observe, you drew them to you by your interference. And now—I sense, Dammy, that you are near to extinction, hurt and alone and without hope. Yet you cheerfully set about rectifying matters to the extent immediately possible. Why, Dammy? Is it merely a desire for death?

I had a funny idea I ought to try to help out a pal, Dammy replied. *And when those birds started taking shots at me, that made it personal. Anyway, they're not so tough. Don't give up. Maybe we can still take 'em.*

Dammy, they're sure to find you soon. By the way, just where are you?

Skip it, Dammy advised the irresolute creature. At that moment he noticed faint sounds in the woods to the east—and to the west and north. Not close; merely a general search pattern, he decided. The right move would be to get inside their ship and play it by ear. He paused a moment to tell Floss of his intentions, showing his former shipmate his position only ninety-eight point-seven-five meters from the guarded entry port, concealed in dense underbrush at the base of a nonesuch tree.

Hang on, he encouraged his fellow victim. *I see you're not tied. How about picking your moment and sneaking away? Maybe I can make a diversion,* he suggested.

Floss replied with a vague negation. *That would only lengthen my torment,* he pointed out.

Now Dammy could hear the approaching Teest horde more clearly. They were closer, the vanguard no more than a hundred yards distant, he observed. He reached out lightly to touch the leader's mind—and failed. His strength, though partially restored, was still far below the level necessary to exercise his full mind powers. For the moment, he abandoned the idea of interfering with the enemy advance and decided instead to concentrate all his strength on reaching the comparative security of the alien ship. It was not excessively difficult to get to his feet, he found, though his newly knitted leg ached severely. He forced his way through the impeding bramblelike growth into which he had fallen, reached open ground. From either side, parties of Teest converged on their vessel, on routes that would bring them very close. He picked the darkest hiding place he could discern, a patch of near total blackness between two major trees. As he entered it, the group on the left bypassed him, squeaking softly among themselves. Dammy changed position, attempting to ease his injured leg. The healing was not complete, he was well aware, it having been carried out with inadequate resources both of energy and molecules. To attempt again to levitate was out of the question; it was challenge enough merely to stay on his feet and conscious. . . .

All around, sounds of heavy boots, crashing of brush, squeals and squeaks. The main body of Teest was passing directly over his position, but so far none had poked into the narrow way between the ancient trees. Then a straggler, pausing to rest, blundered almost against Dammy, halting less than one meter distant to snuffle audibly, testing the air. Dammy listened to its wheezing breathing. After twenty-seven minutes and three point six-eight seconds it moved on. Cramped in the close darkness, Dammy found his thoughts wandering. Suddenly oppressed by the pressure of the warm and humid air, the claustrophobic closeness of the great buttresses of living wood hemming him in, as well as the agony of his leg, he shifted position. At once the departing Teest swerved back toward his place of concealment but, seeing nothing, moved on. Dammy fought to keep his thoughts clear. If he could hold on until this crowd was gone, then he had a chance of doing a nifty sneak around left end, and then—well, after that, he conceded, it looked a little dubious. If he only had a steak and about a quart of good Bavarian beer. . . .

The question, he realized after half an hour of exceedingly complex calculations, was whether the expense of psionic energy necessary to synthesize food from the nearby matter would kill him before he could eat it. But being squeezed in here with no decent air to breathe wasn't making him any money, he informed himself sternly. And how can man die better than facing fearful odds. . . ?

He had to try. The technique was easy enough: just a little straightforward intramolecular rearrangement. The local nucleic acids weren't the ones Terran life used, but they were close relatives. Just stick on an N here and there and get rid of some of those excess S's and K's, and he was in business. He started with the woody material nearest to hand. It was tantalizing to know exactly what to do and how, and to be just a little too weak to do it. He withdrew his forces from all peripheral functions, concentrated on the problem of nudging that damned 0^2 over *that* way. . . . Ah, there it went, clicked into place slick as a whistle. He erected a simple system field of the kind used in routine manufacturing and arranged the forces so as to feed the source molecules at optimum rate into the stress pattern and swiftly aggregate a usable product mass, drawing on available plant cell energies to spare his own waning forces; then he let the process run. After ten minutes he bestirred himself sufficiently to scan the focal *situs*, a nine hundred-cubic-inch hollow in the tree trunk beside him which had served as the source for the withdrawal of material to feed his synthesis. There, on a paper plate—he could have had Spode, or a silver tray, but why bother?—rested an eight-ounce hamburger, nicely broiled, with the appropriate condiments, all on a butter-toasted onion bun. The aroma was heavenly until he discontinued it as wasteful. Before grabbing it, he lifted the silica mug beside it and took a large, healing draught of cold beer.

"Würzburger Hofbräu!" he said, almost aloud. "My favorite—and I didn't even specify. . . . There's a lot more to this than plain old objective matter and energy," he concluded. "I really don't know what kind of forces I'm messing with, but I'll eat first and figure it out later."

Dammy restrained his impulse to take the sandwich in two gulps, instead forced himself to chew and swallow slowly, savoring the flavor of the hickory-broiled beef, noting as he did that had he been any weaker, he would have been unable to eat. He devoted a moment to calculating the relative efficiencies of this method versus direct transport of nutrients to the tissues. The pleasure of eating, he decided, outweighed the slightly greater effectiveness of the latter method.

The crash of underbrush near at hand brought him back to more immediate matters. He saw a pair of gray-clad Teest a dozen meters distant, looking alertly about. They had come, Dammy noted, from the direction of the ship, so it appeared a fine-grid search was under way. Then he caught a glimpse of flower-like color in the gloom beside the Teest: the bedraggled wings of Floss. Dammy saw his former companion more clearly as he and his escort stepped into a small patch of clear ground. They moved without urgency, it seemed to Dammy, the two intruders well in advance, Floss trailing casually as if out for a stroll with friends. The Teest nearest Floss spoke to him: a prolonged squeal. Both Teest probed the surrounding underbrush with sharp glances, aided by their glowsticks. One turned away; then Floss seemed to look straight into Dammy's hidey-hole.

Make a break, Dammy suggested. *Get clear and use your wings.* Floss stiffened and spoke briefly in their own tongue to his escort, gazing toward Dammy's concealment. Then his eyes fixed, seemed to stare directly into Dammy's. He plucked at the sleeve of the nearer Teest and pointed—at Dammy. The two Teest at once concentrated their light beams on his niche and advanced. One idly scorched the foliage around Dammy, a hint of the fiery blast he would receive if he made an incorrect move.

Thanks, pal. Dammy tossed the thought sardonically at Floss, who followed close on his captors'—or friends'(?) heels.

But, Dammy, the distressed reply came, *they*

were hurting me. There was only one thing of value to them that I could offer: you.

So that makes it all OK, Dammy replied. *You're some guy, Floss. Too bad you don't have the guts of a butterfly, even if you do look like one.*

Then Dammy struck at the advancing Teest, a single well-focused mind-thrust. The creature stumbled, let fall its light-weapon, and dropped to all fours. The other backed a step, started to bring his weapon into play, then dropped it and bolted. Dammy stepped out, picked up the gun, and brushed past Floss.

Dammy! What are you—you can't! the distraught informer thought confusedly. Dammy paused to look scornfully at him. *Go back to what's left of your house*, he commanded. *Sit tight and wait for what happens.* Ignoring the quadrupedal Teest, which ambled in an awkward plantigrade gait across his path, he headed for the enemy ship, now bathed in lights.

Eight

The disconcerting chartreuse sunlight glinted from the repolished bubble dome perched on its spider—or butterfly legs above the once again immaculate violet lawn. Dammy stretched and yawned. He felt pleasantly tired after his night's work, and looked forward to testing the beds in the bubble house. Floss appeared on a tiny balcony ledge above, his wings now perfectly groomed and iridescent across the spectrum as the sunlight struck them.

Dammy, he called silently. *Can it be you? As you see, I'm quite well, and*—His excited twittering broke off as a lone Teest appeared from behind a flowering shrub near Dammy, a pruning hook in one hand and a trowel in the other. Dammy touched him gently, recognized him as the first of the aliens whose minds he had adjusted, found serenity in place of the former maelstrom of fears and hungers. The wound was healing nicely.

It's all right, Dammy reassured Floss. *All the rest are aboard ship. Minf stayed to tidy up. He's going now.*

Goodbye, Minf. Dammy placed the salutation

carefully in the confused creature's mind as it hesitated, unsure of what to do and still amazed at the concept of its own individuality. It moved off, silently murmuring its name, its incredible very-own personal *name*.

Once again, Floss stated with satisfaction, *Cosmos has manifested Himself.*

It was no miracle, Dammy said. *Just good old-fashioned force.*

That we met, Floss amplified, *was a manifestation of the Cosmic equilibrium. Though of course your description of the mechanics of the salvation of Almione is interesting to a student of material manipulation. The most delightful aspect of Cosmos is His novelty. Who would have dreamed of the destructive energies of the rapacious Teest turned in a trice to construction. . . ?*

I'm glad they got everything put back in shape, Dammy said. *Looks nice.*

Except for my thousand-year-old heo tree, Floss mentioned sadly. *Yet I have the timber, nicely sawed and stacked, and ten new saplings in place—so even that was not without its place in the pattern. In no other way,* he added, *would I have in my lifetime come upon a supply of the fire-colored heo wood for working. Ah, to see the bright shavings curling amid the aroma of pepper-and-salt, and the glow of the finished piece under my hand!* His inscrutable bee-face turned to Dammy. *And yet, I still don't understand—you, Dammy. Why did you trouble yourself? Why are you here now, concerned for my welfare? It is without logic.*

Never mind, Dammy urged. *I just did what came naturally when I saw a pal in trouble.*

Pal, Floss echoed. *Almost I grasp the concept—a fragile one, but with its own strange inner logic. Or, no, not logic, but a consistency with Cosmos. Yes. That gives me—almost—an insight. And I see that to you, my perfectly logical act in selling you to the torturers in return for a dubious amnesty appeared as strange as your loyalty did to me. Yet now are we reconciled. And what will you do next, Dammy, my . . . friend? Indeed, I hope that I can be rehabilitated in your estimation.*

No hard feelings, pal, Dammy reassured the irresolute creature. *I'll be hitting the road now. I got stuff to do.*

Dammy, Floss said at last, *There is that which I must tell you—as a pal, you understand.*

Yeah?

This person Xorialle of whom you tell me has misinformed you. Yes, of course you drew upon the library as well for your briefing, but it was, after all, this same Xorialle who had programmed the reference stacks. What you know of the Galaxy is, in its main outline, quite accurate, of course; he distorted only what was apropos his purpose—specifically, the impression he deliberately created of the Galactic Concensus as a mighty Galactic power before which all lesser jurisdictions bow the knee. This is false. The Galactic Concensus is the name given by its enthusiasts to a small, disputatious organization bent on arranging affairs along the lines your mentor so ambitiously outlined. It exists precariously, being deemed too trivial a nuisance to warrant extirpation by the mighty ones of the Galaxy. I trust this news does not unduly distress you—nor should it, as I understand your resentment at your proposed 'classification.'

I thought it was a bit strange that the Teest were running around loose inside Concensual space, Dammy said indifferently. *So going to Trisme won't solve anything after all.*

Why not remain here at Almione? Floss proposed. *You may choose as large a tract of virgin territory as you like and transform it to meet your vision.*

Beats me, Dammy said. *But I've still got a feeling that there are things that want me to do them, so I'll hit the trail.*

I see you have little patience with ceremony, Floss said. *Still, after all our adventures together, it seems—*

For just an instant, Dammy felt impalpable forces touch him. Then he was back—aboard the featureless prison capsule he had shared with Floss. Now he was indeed alone.

In the strange, timeless time that followed, Dammy tried with little success to assimilate the experiences of the last six weeks (Terran time). Already Floss and the pathetic Teest seemed remote, and Xorialle and his luxurious prison were like some story heard in childhood and only half-remembered. Before that, there had been—but that part was meaningless, like the dartings of fish in a cloudy bowl. Time, he perceived with shocking clarity, was an illusion imposed by the human mind on its perception of external reality. *Like the Teest,* Dammy thought, *we humans have been fighting ourselves and thinking we were at war with the Universe, when really it's all so sweet.*

Simple and sweet. I thought "work" was a dirty word and spent my life avoiding it, when it's the best there is: to do a job well and know you're doing it. . . .

Suddenly self-conscious, he felt amusement at the philosophic turn his thoughts had taken and deliberately turned his attention to other matters.

"Stuck again," he mused aloud, somewhat startled at the crudity of his native dialect after so many weeks of communication with Floss. "Back in the box where I was before I started poking my fingers in the machinery." He remembered the nightmare struggle across the great swamp with Floss and wondered if he had that to do again. He relaxed on the floor and began to probe his surroundings. Things were changed, he realized at once. Someone had done a tight job of overhauling the shaped energy vessel—if it *was* the same one from which he had escaped before. Now he found no plane of permeability; the stress interlocks were well and truly aligned. He withdrew, and a moment—or a week—later, the iris dilated to deliver the familiar nourishment container, which he emptied directly into his stomach. At last, bored, he turned again to the evocation of the phantom companions who had helped to while away his last period of imprisonment: A room crudely built of packing boxes and rough-sawn logs. A saloon, it seemed, ornamented with the stuffed head of a malemute over the tarnished mirror above the bottle-lined backbar. A crowd filled the room with a din of voices and clumping of muddy boots. Gas lights glared. A bitter wind searched through the many chinks. Dammy noticed the outside temperature was fifty below zero, Fahrenheit. At one side of the saloon, a youthful fellow with a careless air was playing a dilapidated upright in a rhythm Dammy recognized as early ragtime. There was a stir as the plank door opened, and a man in a filthy wolfskin parka came in blinking. His face was pale and hollow, scarred by frostbite; he walked unsteadily, not like a drunk but like an invalid. He went directly to the bar and upended a small, soft-leather pouch, spilling a gleaming mound of yellow sand on the worn boards.

"The stranger's buying," a mouse-faced little man exclaimed, and rushed forward to claim his. Dammy relaxed in his chair against the wall. The piano player was at the bar. The newcomer went to the abandoned piano, threw off his parka, sat heavily on the stool, and swayed for a moment as if about to fall off before he steadied himself and reached purposefully for the keyboard with his gnarled hands. His leather shirt was, if possible, dirtier than the parka. But he could play, Dammy acknowledged as the *Warsaw Concerto* boomed out. No one seemed to pay much attention to the music, though the painted whore at the far table stared across at the stranger's back with an expression of surprise. After a while he finished up and stood, a little steadier now. He turned and made what seemed to be some sort of announcement in a mumble, ended with a word something like 'Damagrue,' Dammy thought as he got to his feet. The stranger had drawn a pistol, and in the same moment that the glare from the chandelier winked out, Dammy realized with astonishment that the gun was aimed directly at him. Even as he started to voice an objection or a question—he wasn't sure which—he felt his right hand twitch, and a double explosion rang out. In the darkness, an impact like Boulder Dam bursting slammed Dammy back and down.

Nine

Dammy awoke remembering: his first aimless probings into the (whatever-it-was) that had surrounded him in the Magic Pumpkin; the abrupt and shocking impact of the presence that had pierced the immaterial walls of his extended awareness, compressing that which was Dammy Montgomerie into a tight-bound point in immensity; and the probing questions. Now again, he realized with dismay, he was under that irresistible scrutiny.

You were warned, being: yet I noted your undisciplined lunge for "freedom" but now. You will receive no further indulgence. Cooperate or cease to exist!

Dammy found this warning encouraging on two counts. First, it suggested that the superintellect which had focused on him was unaware of his foray into freedom with Floss; and second, by repeating its warning of impending punishment rather than carrying it out, it revealed itself capable of inconsistency and irresolution.

So it's only human—sort of, Dammy reassured himself. *It can goof again. But right now I'd better play good.*

I have checked the curious reference you gave me—Sol Three and all that, the substanceless voice spoke again. *I find a curious inconsistency in the record here. The life-form is, after all, known. I have, indeed, a specimen on file, though the specifications differ insignificantly.*

"Oh, boy," Dammy enunciated clumsily in English, with mock enthusiasm. "Back to specimen status. I'm not getting ahead very fast out here in the Big World."

Over the next hours, it was Dammy's impression that the gigantic presence which had seized and questioned him gradually lost interest and idly released its confining pressure. In relief at the surprising realization of his renewed freedom of intellectual movement, he extended his awareness cautiously, sweeping a sector of circumambient whateveritwas—not exactly space-time as postulated by Terrestrial physicists, he noted; more like an infinite manifold of where-whens. But the point was, after all, academic, he reminded himself. He noticed the position of his home system—good old Sol, a remote speck off *there* somewhere—as well as that of Trisme, his intended destination before IT had grabbed him.

You may think of me as Astrobe, the vast intellect informed him abruptly as from a great distance. *I find I have no use for another random item; accordingly, you are free to proceed with your own infinitely trivial affairs.*

Dammy stuck out his tongue, thumbed his nose, and also made rude gestures, enjoying for a moment the feeling of irresponsibility. Then, businesslike again, he expanded awareness to monitor a sphere fifty-one light-years in radius, took a moment to set up an automatic scanning pattern, and turned his thoughts to his next move.

I busted out of Xorialle's coop—or he let me go—all full of big ideas. Now it looks like the problem is getting anyone to use 'em on. Floss was a lightweight. The Teest were just dumb hoods, about like Maxie and Ferd back in Chi. And Astrobe's out of my league in the other direction. So I'll head on in for Trisme and see how much of my briefing on the Galactic Concensus wasn't hot air.

Realigning the transfer capsule's tension matrix left him feeling totally exhausted. He transferred the available nourishment from sphere storage into his digestive tract and experienced a slight belly-ache.

"Eating too fast," he cautioned himself aloud, and respaced the nutrient molecules for optimum assimilation. Then, on impulse, he called:

Hey! Astrobe! Wait a minute! I just happened to think: I've got a few questions of my own. The answer was faint.

It is curious to reflect that such monumental insolence could arise spontaneously from the interaction of certain mildly complex molecules associated in what these selfsame molecules have named "protoplasm." Curious indeed—sufficiently curious to pique my own curiosity. Very well, then, micro-being: what boon would you crave of me?

Well, how about this one? Dammy returned spiritedly. *Tell me what this is all about—why you're messing in my business in the first place. You a traffic cop? And if so, what rule have I broken?*

You may think of me, in homely terms, as a tidy householder noticing a fly in the room.

Yeah? Well, what right do you have to try to swat me?

Right? Hmm. I am of course familiar with the manifestations of energy in its many forms, including the matters, and the interactions thereof, but right is a concept of a surprising subtlety to arise from such a one as yourself. I must examine it further. I choose to forgive your astounding insolence on the basis of your still more astounding ignorance.

Dammy let it go at that.

This time I'll play it smart, Dammy assured himself, noticing that he had formed a habit of talking silently to himself and listening intently for the answers. But he dismissed the matter as a normal response to prolonged idleness and solitude, easily corrected once he was back among people. *If you can call 'em people,* he reflected, thinking of the manifold outré life forms which normally thronged the Great Market at Trisme. He set aside one hundred and two seconds of intense introspection to review the Concensual dialects through C-30, as well as the most widely understood provincial tongues. Ready, he directed the vessel to enter the regulation approach pattern. There was no sensation of change in velocity or direction, but at last (two hundred and thirty-one point six seconds later, Dammy noticed idly) a single, unmodulated *chime!* broke the stillness. Nothing else. Dammy was tensed, ready—for what? He swiftly reviewed the lore in his memory and recalled that for a category twelve VS transport capsule in mode orynx (nonscheduled) all approach and docking maneuvers were handled by Nexus directly. Ergo, he had merely to wait patiently until the capsule was disconstituted in accordance with current energy conservation directives.

But suppose I use the time cooking up something in reserve? Dammy proposed. *Right,* he agreed at once. *Let's see . . .*

Ten

Having decided that it would be wise to be as inconspicuous as possible at first, Dammy studied the texture of his imprisoning walls, found the former stress fields inert now, having reverted to mere matter of approximately the permeability of primitive eighteen-inch naval armor plate. Scanning externally, he detected the presence of half a dozen living beings, the sole occupants of the half-mile-wide parabolic dome within which his vessel had come to rest. He selected the wall opposite the position of the waiting party of six and deftly eased through into echoing darkness and paused to rest. Exercise of his ability to place his material atoms in resonance with barrier materials and then slip through them, he had discovered, not only depleted his chemical-energy reserve very rapidly, but also made his bones itch. He devoted a moment to a cursory examination of the dome, noting that it was two hundred thirty-five point-seven-six-eight meters in diameter at its base, seventy-four point-six-three-two high at its apex, and composed of an alloy of matter and raw energy which would defy his technique of penetration.

Ergo, a door was needed. He found one, an elliptical "soft" spot hidden in the far shadows where heaped bales lay apparently awaiting loading. He felt a gentle *plop!* as the capsule which had imprisoned him for so many weeks and carried him so far (fifteen and a half lights, he noted) dematerialized at his back. At once sounds of activity there directed his attention to the group which had clearly been awaiting him. They were tall, lean, big-eyed creatures armed with wicked scimitars and clad in dirty silks of bile yellow and soiled maroon. They spread out to form a semicircle around the man who crouched in apparent shock at the spot which had been the center of the "floor" of the now vanished capsule.

"Hold it, fellows," the man called in a voice which to Dammy sounded indescribably crude and harsh, though curiously familiar. "I'm here to report a kidnapping. A Vocile Napt, I think it was—that was at first, then this other character—Astrobe, he calls himself—stuck *his* oar in—and there was a gang of Teest running around loose out in Vang Sector. It looks like Concensual authority is going to pieces like a wet sugar cookie."

The stranger swaggered forward, apparently ignoring the menacing gestures of his reception committee. As one approached too closely, he casually caught its drawn sabre by the unsharpened edge and twitched it from the grasp of its owner, who at once turned to his fellows for redress of this impudence. The six uniformed Trismans conferred briefly; then one stepped forward, pointedly sheathing his cutlass as a symbol of truce.

"Look, fellow," he said in a tone of weariness.

"We got a job to do, see? OK, we're down here on a kind of slow guard detail and the word comes through on hot stuff coming in—so we're stuck with it, all in a day's work. Nothing personal, OK? So play it smart and come on down to the shop and talk, and you get off easy."

Dammy covered the last few feet to slip in among the bales and watched as the phantom figure he had evoked as a decoy confronted his would-be captors. A jaunty figure he was, Dammy conceded to himself—swaggering in his red derby, his white silk body shirt with decorative one-inch pearl buttons and black bow tie, the handsomely tailored lapelless jacket.

"What's this all about?" Dammy's simulacrum demanded truculently, seeming not to notice the Trismans edging offside to his left and right.

"You birds never learn," the cop sergeant said. "You keep getting the same big idea you can smuggle contraband farfweed right into Trisme Central and do the state out of its cut of the dope action. So you're under arrest. Turn around and bend over and grab your tarsals and hang on!"

"I guess I got a few rights," the false Dammy countered.

"Damn few," the noncom agreed. "Name one."

"I refer you to the Raptate Code, Section IX, paragraph 91, subsection c: 'In all instances where a breach of the code is presumed solely on the basis of objective exocosmic circumstances, the accused shall have the options of employing counsel of its own designation, or of remaining mute during examination (addendum 44 applies).' "

"Geeze, a guardhouse lawyer," the sergeant almost moaned. "Turning a nice clean little pinch into a like interplanetary incident and all." He waggled his tubelike head and approached as the two flunkies closed in unobtrusively from the sides. Their intended victim casually tossed up the cutlass he had taken from his first challenger, caught it by the hilt, and spun in time to intercept a vicious cut from the left. With a flip he disarmed the creature, which scuttled back as the intended arrestee turned easily to prick the exposed thorax of the right-hand attacker as he raised his blade high. The weapon fell with a tinny clatter and Dammy's double kicked it away.

"Better get yourself some new boys, *Herr Obergefreiter*," he said to the sergeant. "These seem to be a little tired." He spun and barked "scat!" at yet another opportunist easing up behind him. The latter jumped as though goosed by a pitchfork and became as inconspicuous as possible. The real Dammy snorted softly and moved toward the door he had spotted before leaving the capsule. As he reached it, it valved open and a pair of aliens of disreputable appearance crowded in. They were trucial wards of the Glamorph, Dammy noticed by the elaborate, if badly corroded, insignia attached to their Class Ten harness. The leader paused to look Dammy over before speaking:

"A new boy on the run, hey? How come Tanver never tipped us?"

"He was too busy, I imagine," Dammy replied coldly, "doing something important like emptying his ashtray."

"How we know you're the guy?" the ward persisted.

"I'm here, ain't I?" Dammy demanded and brushed past and out into cold gray light and a fine mist that was not quite a drizzle. A hulking lout peered down at him from the driver's perch of a vehicle with an uncanny resemblance to a 1913 Mack Commercial—wagon wheels, solid tires, and all. It was painted a bleary dark green, with mud-obscured lettering in the Pandex script which Dammy translated as "Municipal Motor Pool—Special Duty," and below, "max ld. 875 units (w)." He found this unenlightening.

"Hey, you," the driver called. "Don't hang around."

"Mind your tone, my man," Dammy replied coolly, and turned away. He was aware of a sound of sudden movement just an instant before the world exploded. *Curious—an earthquake without even a premonitory rumble*, he was thinking as he noticed that at a depth of five hundred meters no sunlight penetrates—thus the gleaming lights adorning the curious sea creatures which swarmed about him, examining the intruder. Dammy struck out gamely, swimming for the surface, hardly noticing the odd fact that he was breathing the deep-sea water quite easily.

" . . . OK, boss?" An untutored voice faded into audibility. "I clobbered this chump on the dome; it looked like the softest part."

"Who is he?" someone asked in badly accented C-5. Dammy levered an eyelid up. The creature which half-squatted, looking down at him, was an obese travesty of a mating between a squirrel and an oyster. Its heavy shell was decorated in bright colors of the puce and Mexican pink family, matching the bedraggled ribbons in its bushy tail.

"He's the mug which you said we was after him," the driver stated sullenly. Behind him, someone was emerging from the still open door. Dammy recognized his simulacrum jauntily leading the six-cop detail.

"Uh-oh, maybe I goofed, boss," the big driver grunted. "That there looks like him, and in good with the fuzz, too."

"Beats me," the boss said indifferently. "You can't count how many tails and arms and antlers and stuff this here one's got, dumped in a pile thataway. You sure you didn't slug him too good, Orf?"

"Mighta," Orf conceded. "Let's get him outa here. If it's the wrong bird, we can drop him off at municipal disposal, like the truck says. Kind of a neat touch at that."

As Dammy was hauled to his feet, his double, about to pass by six feet away, checked and approached.

"See here, my man," he said briskly to Orf. "Are you chaps aware you're in the presence of a third lieutenant of the Iowa National Guard?"

"Who, you, sir?" Orf inquired as one eager to please, and snapped to eight feet of slovenly attention.

"By no means, fellow. I myself am a senior attaché of the Triarchy of Gree. *This* personage"—pointing at Dammy—"is the lieutenant. Better get on the ball fast, before he notices you and depilates you on the spot."

Orf and the boss released Dammy at once, allowing him to slump back to the sidewalk, which, he noted, was nicely finished in Yalcan tilework.

"All right, you swine, clear out of there!" an authoritative voice barked.

"Sarge, that's the notorious footpad and cut-purse, Orf," another spoke up, "—and unless I'm much mistook the other miscreant is the Upright Man hisself!"

"Better beat it before I run you in," the cop three-striper said without conviction; but Orf and his employer scrambled quickly aboard the garbage truck and moved off in a cloud of unburned hydrocarbons. A small crowd of curious passersby had gathered. Dammy stared back. They were a varied group—tall and short, shaggy and hard-shelled, in every color of the spectrum, some goggling stemmed eyes, others waving elaborate snoof organs, chattering in a dozen tongues which Dammy had some difficulty in sorting out and interpreting.

". . . one of them Flanches, I bet! I heard—"

". . . notorious dope ring. Degenerate-looking fellow."

". . . over so's a guy can see, for Foob's sake!"

The cops got busy shooing off the audience, then turned back to Dammy, who by now had managed to control his head's tendency to expand and contract by a factor of ten with each pulsebeat.

"Hey, sarge," he called. "Wasn't that Orf, the notorious footpad, you just turned loose?" He got to his feet, swaying only a little, braced himself against the wall.

The cops, happy now with a familiar routine to occupy them requiring no exercise of their limited thought power, glowered at the last departing eyeballer and turned back to their sergeant for approval. The latter was glumly eyeing Dammy.

"What was that crack, lootenant?" he demanded, advancing holding in his pudgy hands a device that was not so intricate that Dammy was unable to recognize it as a form of handcuff.

"Mind your tone, my man," Dammy replied coolly. "Now you may report to me. Exactly what were your instructions regarding your mission here at the depot today?"

"Well," the noncom said, "all we got was, a nonsched vital support transfer encapsule with contraband was going to do a sneak docking at locus 12-137251A at two bells sharp, and we was to put the arm on the bum which he swiped the can from some big-shot bureaucrat. And you hit it right on the button."

"I see," Dammy replied. "In other words, a simple case of mistaken identity due to an otherwise commendable excess of zeal."

"Yeah, I guess," the chastened cop said, reluctantly reholstering the cuffs. "Well, boys," he addressed his minions, "I guess we better be reporting in on a dry run, which we done our best."

As the abashed flatfeet shuffled their service boots and lined up, Dammy's simulacrum pushed through them to confront the sergeant.

"Look here, you dumb hick cop," he said impatiently. "How about apologizing to this nobleman and offering him class A transport to his destination—and make it snappy!"

"On the other hand," the boss cop said, "any pinch is better'n no pinch at all. So—" he turned to Dammy, again unlimbering his cuffs, which, Dammy noted, operated on a nerve-pinch principle which rendered the restrained members permanently semi-operable. He stepped back.

"Hey!" the cop said. "You know, you two bums do look kinda alike. To a untrained optic organ, I mean. Like you both got pink bowler hats, only yours got a dent in it—that's on account of Orf cold-cocked you one," he elucidated. "C'mere, mug."

"Now, officer," (the real) Dammy said placatingly. "There's been another misunderstanding. You were dispatched here to intercept contraband, not to harass officials of a friendly power. As you know, Iowa and Trisme have always accorded Most Favored Nation status, reciprocally, to each other."

"Naw, I never went in fer that diplomacy stuff," the cop demurred. "Being a cop is crooked enough for *me*."

"Smarten up, copper," Dammy's double advised sharply, ignoring Dammy's hand signals to shush. "Round up your morons and beat it."

"You, again, huh?" the sergeant replied, and turned to look him over. "Hey, which one of you guys is which, anyways?" he inquired feelingly.

"I'm the good one," Dammy said promptly. Behind the sergeant's back he removed his hat and, as the cop turned, deftly traded with his self-copy. The cop waggled his head sadly. "I thought it was *him* with the dent in his dome," he said aggrievedly.

"It *was;* I mean it is," Dammy reassured the lawman. "Better grab him quick."

The cop nodded and advanced, this time on the false Dammy. He paused, fingering his restraining device with increasing indications of frustration. "Lousy issue bracelets," he commented. "OK., fella, I decided to give ya a break and not put the cuffs on ya. You gonna come along nice?"

"Forget it, dummy," his intended victim replied. Dammy stepped forward. "Perhaps I can be of assistance, officer," he said, and plucked the malfunctioning device from the cop's hands. With a deft motion and a twist of the wrist, he apparently turned the device inside out and handed it back. "I think you'll find it operative now," he said offhandedly.

"Hey, why'ncha say you was one of the boys, brother?" the policeman inquired genially. "I guess you was having a few yocks, hey?" He offered a hopeful chuckle.

"Sure, brother," Dammy said soothingly.

"Wait'll I take care of this wise guy, which it looks like he was figgering to pass hisself off as you, sir, the slob." The cop deftly clamped the restraining device, neuronic, Mark IV, 1.N 76842, on the unresisting simulacrum.

"Good work, captain," Dammy said. "Watch him closely. He looks tricky."

"Don't worry none about this boy. I never had nobody break from me yet, once I got the old Mark IV on him."

At that instant the simulacrum disappeared with a faint *plop!* of imploding air. The cuffs fell to the pavement. For a moment Dammy felt curiously lightheaded. *Gotta eat,* he thought.

"I was just gonna put the cuffs on the bum," the sergeant announced unhappily, retrieving his Mark IV, "and he knees me and does a snappy dive into a waiting car, which beats it in a hurry. Probably a plant!"

"Sure, sergeant," Dammy commiserated. "He took advantage of your good nature."

"Maybe I'm slipping my clutch." The sergeant looked worried.

"By no means, major. Excuse me for a moment while I meditate. I feel the need of a brisk stroll to stimulate the circulation," he added. Without waiting for formal permission, Dammy set off toward the corner, where he encountered Orf with his garbage truck.

"Good show you didn't make the turn," Dammy said. "There's a detail of coppers planning an ambush right in front of the main cargo dome."

"Them sneaky flatfeet!" Orf spat. "I got you now," he added. "You're Slick Slunt, the notorious cutpurse and footpad and all."

"Right!" Dammy agreed. "Can you tell me where to find the action in this burg?"

"Can I! You know me, Slick—always in touch. Besides, the boss likes a little action, too."

"Swell. Let's go—but on second thought, let's have a little fun with the precinct boys first. There's a pretty sharp sergeant and six beat-pounders hiding behind the shrubbery next to the employees' entrance."

"Yeah, but there ain't no shrubbery around there."

"Right. Makes 'em easy to spot. Just pull in slow, like you were going to stop—then gun it. I'll meet you later on—you say where."

The sergeant was shaking his head mournfully as Dammy sauntered back.

"I blew it, brother," he said. "The bum pulls a caper right here in broad daylight. Looks like maybe it's time for me to turn in my badge."

"Don't feel bad, chief. You couldn't help it if

you had a couple bad breaks. I'll put in a good word for you with the commissioner."

"Geeze, would you, pal? Say, I guess maybe it's lucky I pulled this detail after all—you know, there's a reason for everything."

"Did you ever hear of a joint called the Green Corpse?" Dammy asked casually on a sudden impulse, wondering why even as he spoke.

"Are you kidding! Sure, you're a guy with a laugh for every occasion. I ain't been around that end o' town since the big Slunt pinch, three cycles back come promotion time. What about it?"

"I heard about the place and thought I'd like to have a look while I'm in town," Dammy improvised.

"Better watch it down there, Your Honor. It's one of them, like, dens of iniquity and all like you hear about. Maybe we shoulda cleaned it up, but it's kind of handy at that; all the crime in town operates outa the dump."

"Good thinking, captain. How about dropping me off?"

"Sure, pal, no trouble—but not before you see the commish, right?"

"Say about stardown?"

"Pick you up right here—or at your hostel, whichever. Believe me, sir, Sergeant Bloot is a cop which he knows a real gent when he sees one—which ain't often. By the way, when you're chinning with your pal the commish, don't say nothing about how that slob which I was picking him up on suspicion broke from me, OK?"

"Not a word," Dammy agreed. *Funny*, he mused. *With all the sophisticated techniques from Machiavelli to Drunt at my disposal, it turns out the best* approach is the good old double cross. I might as well be back in Chi.

Without warning, it came sweeping in from a great distance: a solid—no, not a solid, not even a gas, Dammy corrected himself—a wall of vibrating molecules, yet not the molecules themselves, but the vibration, well down in the sonic range, though with sub- and supersonic harmonics. It was, in fact, a sound, he belatedly realized, filling all of time and space.

Oh, the Big Bang, so it must be true after all, he had time to think before it caught him up, swept him off into depthless immensity where he hung motionless, spinning rapidly on his long axis and rotating around a radiant body nearby at an infinite distance.

So now I'm a planet, he said to himself silently in a voice that boomed away to the retaining wall of eternity and bounced back as a faint squeak.

Let's get it together, Montgomerie, he commanded himself sternly. Now there was smoke, dense and black and choking, if he had happened to be breathing, plus a curious sensation of being tied to an anchor off *there* somewhere. At last he identified it: pain. A curious concept. Why should pain be regarded as unpleasant? And what was pleasure?

Yet it seemed important to check on it. He hauled on the monomolecular filament linking him to it and came sailing in through dizzying vistas of exploding galaxies, deftly dodging the rubble to come to rest at last with a mind-numbing impact. He clutched, found sharp spikes and broken glass, let go, and slid—to smash up against that which encompassed him like a downy water bed filled with gentle dreams. He blinked and opened his eyes.

A deep amber dusk filled the narrow street like a high tide of orange pekoe, but the phosphorescent chartreuse signboard marking the location of the Green Corpse was unmistakable. For once, "You can't miss it" had been no exaggeration. Few pedestrians lingered in the Street of the Bad Smell—for many reasons, Dammy realized, in addition to the one celebrated in the name. Dammy passed two lean, pale blue Evian prostitutes standing in a deep doorway, swerved aside to avoid a lumbering Truncan aristocrat accompanied by a bodyguard of four spidery Theel. A lone Trisman loitered near the open entry of the dive which was Dammy's appointed rendezvous. After dropping him at the foot of the street, Sergeant Bloot had departed in haste, mentioning reports to complete, Dammy remembered, as if from another lifetime.

As Dammy came up, he flicked a thought at the apparently casual Trisman by the doorway from which issued sounds and smells suggesting both mirth and violence. The guard eased into Dammy's path.

"Routine check, sir," the doorman buzzed in a gutter variant of C-5.

"Out of my way, scum!" Dammy buzzed back.

The fellow advanced menacingly. Dammy held his ground. The watchman's hand began to stray toward his hip. "Want to try me, punk?" he snarled.

Remembering the techniques of Fast Harry the Dip, Dammy shot out his hand, plucked the gun from the thug's pocket, dropped the magazine from the butt, fired the chambered round into the air, and replaced the weapon before the magazine struck the oily cobbles.

Down the block, the Theel bodyguards had clustered close around their patron and were gazing toward the encounter in the doorway. The guard, struggling to retain his aplomb, waved them on.

"Just a gag, boys," he called, then returned his gaze to Dammy.

"I hope I didn't see that," he muttered.

"Go inside and reserve me the best table in the house," Dammy ordered curtly. "And hot up the biggest and best steak in Trisme."

"Who'd you say you was?" The Trisman inquired anxiously, edging toward the entry.

"Tell 'em Groucho sent you," Dammy replied. "And put some snap into it."

Five minutes later Dammy's knife sliced through a crusty brown-black exterior into the deep pink middle of a two-inch slab of gently steaming loin of blurb-beast. He noticed that his hands trembled slightly. Although he had conserved energy by manually disarming the doorman rather than merely teleporting the gun from his pocket, he was almost at the end of his strength. One more show of resistance by the guard, he knew, would have finished him.

The steak was superb. Its weight, Dammy noted, was thirty-eight-point-one ounces. Just right. The flavor was indistinguishable from that of U.S. prime porterhouse, and there was less bone. Idly he wondered how a herd of blurb-beast would fare on a big spread in Texas or Florida—eight hundred pounds of beef each, plus a superb pink-and-yellow hide for tanning.

Intent on his much needed meal, Dammy had ignored as far as possible the noisy polyglot mob that thronged the wide, low dining and gaming room. His steak finished, he was aware of a euphoric sensation of renewed vitality. Relaxing comfortably in his chair, toying with a thin-walled glass of black wine, he looked around, amusing himself by identifying the various types previously familiar to him only via Xorialle's briefing tapes. The variety was astonishing, but, he reminded himself, actually no more so than that to be observed among little Terra's two million species of extant arthropods alone, to say nothing of the other great phyla, plus the flora. Nature, clearly, was inexhaustible in her solutions to the problems of manning the interface between the animate and the inanimate. A glimpse of rainbow color caught his eye.

"Floss!" he called against the hubbub. At once the attentive Anciloid waiter was at his side, solicitous. Dammy reassured him.

"Just spotted an old pal and yelled without thinking," he explained, and pointed out the fragile figure at the center of a crowd of relatively drably attired Trismans. The waiter bobbed his carrot-shaped head and hurried away. A moment later, Dammy looked up to see the familiar, thin, gorgeously colored, bee-faced, butterfly-winged form of his old ship- and cellmate. "Sit down, Floss," he urged. "Fancy meeting you here, as the saying goes."

"I fear, sir, there's been an error," the anxious waiter interposed. "This being, sir, is his Excellency Field Marshall General Baron Clace, honoring this humble establishment with a visit on the occasion of his accession to his titles and position at the Board." He went on to introduce Dammy as the Lord Bongbong, just in from Zrade on Syndicate business; then he withdrew, to leave Dammy looking quizzically at the colorful alien.

"Lord Boom-boom, that's me," Dammy said. "Alias Slick Slunt."

"I understood the fellow to say Bong-bong, milord," the butterfly creature chimed.

"Just a slip of the brain, I guess, Floss," Dammy replied. "Sit down and try this vintage. It's not bad. Not good, but not bad."

"As the menial informed you, milord, I am Baron Clace," Floss said with a single, sharp, plucked-string tone. "Kindly disabuse yourself of the notion that I am some sort of crony of your lordship. I fear I've not previously had the honor."

"Knock it off, Floss," Dammy said genially as he flicked out a quick mental probe to contact the familiar, vaguely defined mind-field of the feckless creature whose life and estate he had saved from the depredations of the fierce Teest horde. To his astonishment, he met an impervious barrier reminiscent of that which had contained both him and his fellow prisoner in the transfer capsule. He laughed, causing the other to wince.

"Pretty cute, Floss," he chimed in Concensual Seven. "What was the idca of playing them so close to your chest?"

The gossamer-winged creature drew out a chair and seated himself. "You must give no indication of familiarity," he *ding!*ed softly. "You are in great danger."

"Sure, aren't we all?" Dammy said gaily. "What's

it all about?" He looked around. While he intercepted no inimical gazes, he felt somehow that all eyes were focused on the byplay at his table. Then three bigger-than-usual Trismans in garments of austere yet elegant cut and color separated themselves from the throng to approach, side by side, until they loomed directly behind Floss—or Baron Clace, as he insisted.

"Oh, a pinch, huh?" Dammy said carelessly. "Another sellout. I wondered how the boys happened to be on the spot to meet me."

"As it happens, milord, I am a ranking officer of Concensual Intelligence," the bee-faced aristocrat stated flatly. "I am merely doing my duty. In fact, I have just saved you from destruction. Had I given a different signal, you would have been burnt on the spot. That was, in fact, Contingency A. But I have reprieved you—temporarily. So much for superfluous explanations. Now—who are you?"

"Knock it off, Floss," Dammy said amiably. "You know I'm Dammy Montgomerie. What's the game?"

"I've told you candidly enough that I am an intelligence officer, Dammy. Am I to reveal all my professional secrets at your demand?"

"Just quit kidding me," Dammy said. "You can admit you're Floss without giving away any weight, since I already know it."

"Very well, Dammy, I did indeed once assume the persona you insist on. You see? I reserve nothing—or almost nothing." The bee face seemed to express pleased expectation of Dammy's satisfaction with this declaration.

"So now you're a big-shot G-man with a small group of enthusiasts, is that the picture?" Dammy said sardonically.

"I don't think I quite understand," Baron Clace replied stiffly.

"You tipped me off—remember? just as a pal—that the Galactic Concensus is a nut bunch that wants to take over the Galaxy with nothing but hot air and big ideas."

"In the course of one's profession, one must at times dissemble, of course," Floss (or Baron Clace) said stiffly.

"Thanks, pal. What was the idea? That I'd stumble in and get swatted before I opened my mouth? And then you tipped the authorities just to be sure."

"It is irrational, Dammy, to attempt to assign values to my actions in accordance with your own twisted views."

"That's OK, Flossie. In fact, you did me a favor; you blew it. If you hadn't gone to the trouble, I might have been a lot slower to realize how important I am to you people."

"I fail to grasp your meaning," Baron Clace said in a single icy tone resembling an eight-pound sledge hitting a chilled anvil.

Dammy signaled to the Anciloid waiter, who had been hovering within range.

"Do it again," Dammy said. "The whole meal—just for desert. After a big blurb steak, there's nothing like another steak to settle the stomach."

Floss declined to order. "You seem to have an excessive appetite, if you'll pardon my mentioning it," he chimed reprovingly. "I myself keep to a strict diet of the Tinc school, mostly floral nectars."

"Kind of light on protein," Dammy said. "No wonder you're so skinny—if you'll pardon my mentioning it." He proceeded to devour his second dinner with excellent appetite. Floss looked on unmoved.

"There are three kinds of hungry," Dammy said expansively. "Type A is social; you like the idea of settling down in a good restaurant with a few buddies and ordering up something special. Then Type B—that's when your stomach says, 'It's time to stuff me again.' Type C is when your cells are a little depleted and need feeding. That's what you get on a good weight-loss diet and what'll kill you if you don't eat. I had all three." He patted his abdomen comfortably.

"Candidly, Dammy, I was astonished that you evaded Lieutenant General Lord Bloot, and High Commissioner Orf's group as well," Close confided briskly. "You unveiled a whole new range of behavior I had not been led to expect. You're crafty, Damocles. I see now that your entire handling of the party of Teest 'vandals' (a picked crew, I assure you) was merely a ploy designed to delude me as to your practicality in policy matters."

"Not entirely. I really did hate to see 'em lousing up your pad. I kind of liked it."

"I should imagine. After all, I extracted the concept from your own third-level fantasies."

"You called me crafty, Floss. But you're quite a subtle operator yourself. I've been wondering what you're up to *now*—and I just figured it out."

"Did you, indeed?" Baron Clace murmured indifferently.

"First," Dammy said, "I noticed that things got very quiet here as soon as you came over to my table; all the spontaneous mayhem faded out. But the skeleton crew of bullyboys hanging around in the corners wasn't watching *me*. They were watching you."

"You delude yourself, Damocles," Floss *ding!*ed. "My minions are of course attentive to my strategies."

"Nuts," Dammy commented. "You're under surveillance, not me. And another thing. The whole play—all that sweet jazz back at the docks, the runaround with Sergeant Bloot, and this setup—it's all supposed to soften me up so I'll sob out my whole story on your shoulder. But why not just run me in and work me over under the lights? You're trying to build up the dependency relationship so you can pump *me*. You think I can tell you what it's all about. Sorry, chum."

The bee-faced alien leaned forward with a show of earnestness. "The Galaxy, Damocles, is infinitely more vast and complex than you imagine. Forces are in flux now which will determine the evolution of Cosmos for unthinkable ages yet to come. Why not simply relax and accept your good fortune in having gained my indulgence?"

"Could you be a little more specific, you two-faced chiseler?" Dammy said in a humble tone. "By the way, one other thing I'm sure of, Baron: you're not so tough."

"I, tough, Damocles?" Floss twitched his wings, which looked almost gray now in the subdued light. "You're quite aware that I in no way fancy myself as a ruffian. I am, rather, a sensitive being oriented toward aesthetics."

"What the farmer stepped in," Dammy said flatly. "Out of all the gunslingers in town, how come they picked *you* to brace me man-to-man at high noon, so to speak?"

When the alien made no answer, Dammy pushed back his chair and rose. "Better slap leather, big boy. The let's-be-pals play didn't work." He reached across the table, put his hand against the shell-hard, bristly velvet-black face and pushed. Floss's chair went over backward. Dammy stepped over the prostrate creature and walked to the door without looking back, reflecting on the curious discovery he had made when he touched the bristly, bee-eyed face.

Eleven

Outside, Dammy paused, felt a momentary dizziness, but recovered himself and went quickly to a reeking alley mouth adjacent to the Green Corpse. He stepped into the shadows and waited to observe as a squad of security men, emerging from the door he had just quitted, closed in on the jaunty figure in the dented pink derby, who bowed with mock courtesy and accompanied them to a waiting paddy wagon. It dug off with a screech and disappeared around a corner. An instant later, a metallic *car-rongg!* shattered the night stillness. From its point of origin, a flash of white light cast sharp shadows across the square. A lone security man came running back to dart inside the Corpse. He reemerged instantly, running even faster. Then Floss came out peering about hesitantly, as if checking for rain.

"Come on, Floss, cut the comedy," Dammy called. "Why not get wise to yourself and quit trying to ace me?"

"To be sure," Floss *pong!*ed. For a moment he seemed a bit confused; then he came briskly across to Dammy. "I acknowledge my error, Damocles," he said in a businesslike way. "I perceive that special tactics will be necessary in dealing with such an anomalous phenomenon as yourself."

"Cool," Dammy grunted. "What have you got planned next? By the way, I give you full points for *savoir faire.* Getting pushed in the mush and knocked on your can would have been enough to rile up just about anybody but you. You didn't miss a line—dumb as the line was. You know the game's up now. But aren't you anxious about why I did it?"

"I assume it was mere ruffianly pique at your failure to intimidate me. Then, of course, my squad men did act precipitately, without awaiting my authorization, which is naturally in contravention not only of regulations, but of my own personal policy."

"So what?"

"Surely, Damocles, you recognize that it is essential that you and I come to an accommodation based on a realistic assessment of affairs."

"Go soak your head," Dammy suggested.

"To what end?" Floss asked seriously. "Oh, I see," he added. "Another of your incomprehensible verbal sallies."

"OK, so far we've established that, for some reason you're being coy about, I'm too important to be allowed to run around loose. I was pretty green, thinking I'd just stumbled onto harmless, simple little old you—and all that jazz about being captured by a Vocile Napt. OK, and now we both know a little better. But I'm still wondering why you had it set up for me and how you knew when and where to nab me. Xorialle must have tipped you after all. I was a trusting soul in those days.

When I saw him using a crowbar on the star radio, I took it at face value—sort of. But where does that leave us now? I'm ready for a good night's sleep and a fresh day. What do you want?"

"I, want, Dammy?" Floss repeated as if astonished. "What could I possibly desire from such as you?"

"Never mind, I've got the answer: what you want is to tie me up with this Keystone Kops routine, but for what? Never mind again," he went on. "I'm a little slow tonight, but I've got to adjust to the idea: you're not running the show, so you're just as mystified as I am."

"Nonsense. I am in complete control of the situation."

"Maybe we ought to join forces and maybe we'll get somewhere."

Clace-Floss uttered a derisive *ping!* and added, "I assure you, my boy—"

"You already assured me," Dammy cut him off. "And I'm definitely not your boy."

"You try my patience sorely," the winged creature said severely.

"All right. I'll be good. I know when I'm overmatched," Dammy said, and at once launched a concentrated probe at the other's mind—and crashed against a steel-hard barrier. He recoiled dizzily, reconstituted his probe, and tried again. This time, an irresistible force caught and contained his probe. A moment later, it burst into his mind and loomed there, almost blocking off thought. Dammy tried in vain to rally his forces.

"Dammit," he sputtered. "They ought to lift old Doc Xorialle's license; the first time I really run up against a problem, I fold like wet Christmas wrappings."

"Don't feel bad, Damocles. You're not yourself—and I mean that quite literally."

"Is that supposed to mean something?" Dammy inquired hazily.

"Think, Damocles," Floss urged mildly. "You have recklessly employed great powers, powers not to be invoked thoughtlessly. Surely you could have suspected, if not deduced, that such abilities come at a price."

"Sure. I always have a big yen for a hamburger right after I pull a big number."

"Not only that. Of course, exercise of psi powers is a massive drain on the physical vitality of the organism, carelessness can easily result in sudden death."

"Now he tells me."

"A pity. Xorialle should have warned you—but of course, he failed to realize fully the degree of success he had actually achieved. But it was irresponsible."

"Sure—but what was that crack about me having a nervous breakdown or something?"

"I said 'you're not yourself,' a figure of speech—usually."

"Come on, get to the point."

"You'll doubtless recall experiencing a moment of disorientation earlier today," Floss suggested.

"A moment? On the level, I haven't been what you could call oriented since I closed the hatch on the Magic Pumpkin back at the North Pole."

"Before abandoning the transfer encapsule, you took what doubtless seemed clever countermeasures in case of a hostile reception: you evoked a fourth-level simulacrum as a decoy."

"Right—and it worked like a charm."

"Such an evocation, Damocles, is perhaps the most dangerous possible form of psi. It was for that reason that it didn't occur to Field Marshall Bloot that you'd employ such a drastic tactic."

"I figured old Bloot was too dumb to be a real sergeant. Anyway, I faked him out of position."

"To be sure. Now think back, Damocles: do you recall any period of, ah, mental blankness, so to speak? A time during which you'd find it difficult to account for your actions?"

"Well, the fact is, things are a little hazy there after Bloot gave me a lift. The next thing that's really clear is when he dropped me here in the street outside the Corpse."

"That period represents a time during which you, as Damocles Montgomerie, did not exist."

"Huh?"

"Had you no qualms when you sent your unprotesting simulacrum off to destruction but now, Dammy? Were we to stroll around the corner, we'd find the charred corpse still chained to its seat in the ruins of the armored car."

"Let's go take a look at the remains," Dammy said. "The boys hustled me into a paddy wagon and drove it around the corner and into a stone wall. It's not often a guy gets to see his own corpse, and I'm not the boy to pass it up. C'mon." He led the way around the corner.

Dammy stood staring at the charred and gutted ruins of the still smoking armored car. "Funny there's no dead cops around," he said. "But I guess that would have been a little stiff even for warmhearted old Floss-Clace-Astrobe."

"It was a foolish scheme—and as you see, it backfired," Floss conceded. "My best computations showed no indication that you would be able to transfer your ego-gestalt to your simulacrum even in the instant of dissolution."

"But why blow me up in the first place? You act as if I was a ticking bomb."

"True enough, Damocles, and the ticking has been proceeding for a very long time. It was necessary to act now. Even incorrect action is preferable to nothing."

"I'm going to do my best to change your mind on that point," Dammy said grimly. "It looks like I'm going to have to bring up the big guns. Let's take a look at the body." He advanced on the heat-radiating mass, a mere tattered shell of steel 178, the gutted hulk resting on heat-deformed wheels in the center of a ring of scorched pavement. At one side, a charred heap lay in the total relaxation of death. Dammy looked down at the blackened face, the smoldering remnants of the once natty outfit clinging to the broken body. He picked up the crushed pink hat and examined it minutely.

"You make it sound pretty cold-blooded. But it was just a simulacrum, remember? Not really loveable old me—or anybody."

"What do you suppose the simulacrum would have said to that, had you asked it—or him?"

"Beats me. Nothing much, I guess. It was like a ghost, you know—or a three-D photo."

"Indeed? How do you feel now, Dammy? Do

you experience the sensation of life? Are you aware of your identity as Dammy Montgomerie?"

"Sure, why not?"

"Because, Damocles, you are the simulacrum."

Hours later, in a wide-windowed office with a view of the metropolis spreading to the horizon, Clace gazed at Dammy sympathetically.

"Think, Damocles," he buzzed. "The Concensus could not long survive if it permitted any placeless being who so wished to flout its laws with impunity. You've not been singled out for unjust persecution. Concensual courts are the culmination of the ideal of justice."

"Swell," Dammy said indifferently. "When do I get to call my lawyer?"

"There is no need for that, Damocles. The court itself represents your interests more perfectly than could any less informed agency."

"Neat. So when do I come to trial?"

"Tsk," Clace-Floss said, "don't trouble your head over that, my boy."

"You've got a six-year backlog or something, I guess," Dammy commented.

"By no means. Concensual courts are as efficient as they are just. Your case has already been tried."

"What's the verdict?"

"Guilty, of course. What else? You know quite well, Damocles, that you've conducted yourself with complete disregard of Concensual law from the moment that you first probed into unauthorized areas back at Xorialle's little installation."

"What's the sentence?"

"I assure you, it won't be mere dull confinement. The Galactic Concensus is an ancient civilization, Dammy. It longs for novelty, for the spectacle of the unknown outcome. You've shown yourself a resourceful being. Just how resourceful will be made apparent, both for the chastisement of you, the malefactor, and for the adumbration of the peace-loving Concensual public."

"Yeah. What's all that supposed to mean?" It seemed to Dammy that perhaps later, when he felt less tired, he might attempt to understand. But at the moment, he was drowsy.

Twelve

"I guess arenas are all the same, from the Circus Maximus to Yankee Stadium," Dammy reflected as he surveyed the structure looming above him. The noisemakers strutted, making noises. Banners rippled in a light breeze.

A pair of iron gates at the far side of the arena opened with a clang. Two Trismans with long poles stood by alertly as *something* came charging from the dark tunnel under the grandstand, plantigrade on four awkward limbs.

At first glimpse, Dammy thought it was a bear. Then, "Nope," he decided, "too skinny, and—"

Next, as the galloping creature slid to a halt and crouched, then sprawled, its dark, shaggy pelt dust-splotched, it seemed to be a man wearing fur long johns.

Dammy advanced cautiously. When he was ten feet from the beast, it stirred; long arms and bowed legs disconcertingly terminating in almost human hands stretched. One foot reached across to scratch with black-nailed fingers at a threadbare patch that Dammy now saw was a less densely furred chest. The creature rolled over onto its back. At the head end, an astonishingly wide mouth opened on large, squarish, lemon yellow teeth and a bright pink buccal cavity where a grayish tongue lolled. Above the mouth were two orifices nearly an inch in diameter, surrounded by whorls and convolutions of what appeared to be gristly black flesh. Still higher, a pair of small, red-edged, and bloodshot brown eyes stared back at him blandly.

"Hey," Dammy said. "It's some kind of big monkey or something. But it has hominid 5-Y dentition. . . ."

Astonishing, a clear but silent voice spoke between Dammy's ears. *Such a freak as this, seeing me in my beauty as a kind of overgrown meepah. It is of the people by its smell, but far gone in sickness, its body bald, its limbs somewhat wasted. It has covered itself in strange skins to hide the shameful disease. But what the hell—company's company.*

Gee, thanks, pal, Dammy thought sardonically. *I guess I'm really in the big time now, being accepted as one of the boys by an overgrown rhesus. Or maybe Australopithecus robustus, to be technical.*

"Hi," he said aloud. The apelike man-thing recoiled and rolled its eyes as if searching for an escape route.

It barked at me, the creature's thought came clearly to Dammy. *I hope it doesn't attack. . . .* The creature extended four empty hands one by one in a tentative way. Dammy gently shook each in turn. The horny palms felt hot and dry and hard, like a dog's paw. The ape-man took this gesture in good part, looking more cheerful now.

"Don't worry, sport," Dammy said soothingly. "I promise not to bite first."

Curious. Sport's reaction came to Dammy not precisely as silent words, but as wordless concepts. *It barks as it speaks. One wonders why. Why do you bark, fellow?*

"Well, I'll tell you, Sport," Dammy said softly. "It's the practice back home these days. By the way, how long have you been in stir?"

Based on the residual percentage of nuclide 152 *I note in my tissues, I estimate . . . um, may I rummage for a unit of measure?* Dammy winced as he felt the ghostly touch inside his skull.

"That's the first time anybody but me ever racked my memory," he commented.

Ah, here we are . . . one million, seven hundred and forty-two thousand, nine hundred and four and one-half, uh, years.

"Almost two million years?" Dammy gasped. "How come you're not dead, Sport?"

I'm a philosophical sort of fellow, I suppose, Sport replied. *I go along from sleep to sleep, meal to meal, getting what pleasure I can from life—and somehow it hasn't yet seemed necessary to terminate.*

"You sound like it was up to you," Dammy said weakly.

I can hardly catch your speech, for your barking, Sport said. *Why not discontinue the barking and let's have a quiet talk, there's a good fellow. And of course it's up to me—what else?*

"Where I come from, most guys live as long as they can, and then they go kicking and screaming."

Seems dreadful, Sport commented. *And where do you come from?*

"How's your astronomy?" Dammy asked bluntly.

Poor. I doubt that I could enumerate the spectral characteristics of more than half the stars in this Galaxy alone.

"I see. Well, here it is." Dammy visualized the location of Sol relative to 61 Cygni, Alpha Centauri, Vega, Capella, Sirius, etc.

Remarkable! Sport commented. *Actually . . . but no, that's unlikely. Still, yes, the Star of the Cold Bride, and the double planet itself! Come to my arms, fellow, diseased or no! We are, it seems, planet-fellows.*

Dammy accepted the man-thing's embrace without enthusiasm.

You hang back, Sport noted. *You're shy—but don't feel inferior, simply because of a physical circumstance. But stay! I can show you quite easily how to re-stimulate the old follicles, and we'll have you as handsome as myself in a trice!*

"Never mind, Sport," Dammy declined. "It's a friendly thought and it does you credit. But I'm saving my strength for the crunch."

You anticipate difficulties? Sport inquired without urgency.

"I've already *got* difficulties," Dammy pointed out. "How about you, Sport? You like being cooped up for two million years?"

You exaggerate, Sport demurred. *Actually I've seen a great deal more of the Galaxy than I would have turning over rotted logs looking for succulent grubs back in good old Here.*

"You're not one of those optimists, are you?" Dammy demanded.

A curious thought, Sport responded. *How can*

one 'look on the bright side,' when every side is so bright?

"I've been trying to figure out what species you are," Dammy confided in Sport. "No doubt about your being Animalia, Chordata, Vertebrata, Mammalia, Eutheria, Primata, Anthropoidiae, but after that it looks kind of dubious. No offense, but nobody's ever dug up a Hominidea with hands on his leg bones."

Umm. Actually, I shouldn't expect the metatarsals would fossilize all that well, was Sport's only comment.

"Two million years," Dammy mused. "That would put you back in the time of *Australopithecus*." He visualized the latter as reconstructed.

Oh, those little fellows. Had one chap who caught a young female and claimed he was keeping her as a pet; then one day she turned up preggers. So they must be a closely related species, though one hates to acknowledge it.

"May I?" Dammy inquired, and extended a sensory feeler to explore Sport's cerebrum.

Go right ahead. I've already studied you, rather rudely, I admit, while you were busy thinking of other matters.

Silently Dammy nodded and proceeded to examine Sport's cortex.

"This is kind of strange," he commented. "Broca's and Wernicke's areas both hypertrophied, and the angular gyrus undersized. I assume that's got something to do with your being a telepath. . . ." He probed further and was astonished to discover an anterior extension of the arcuate fasciculum to a well-developed patch of the cortex for which no specific function was known.

"We're wired up a bit differently," he told his cellmate. "But I guess you wouldn't know much about anatomy."

No more than I do of astronomy. I noticed your curiously withered speech areas, and I assume the oddly truncated fasciculum is responsible for your odd habit of barking as you speak.

"Funny idea," Dammy replied. "Early man was telepathic, and evolved away from it. I wonder why?"

Perhaps I can explain that, Sport offered. *We were having a difficult time with ogres and trolls—great ugly devils they were, just people-looking enough to make them all the more repulsive. Used to jump us unexpectedly and kill all they could and then eat the corpses' brains. So we began to employ a barking code which, of course, they couldn't interpret. Perhaps in time it became the chief mode of speech. Yet you speak well enough.*

"I'm an unusual case," Dammy said. "I was picked out for special training."

I note the larynx has descended, as well as the lingual attachment, Sport said. *Makes barking easier, I suppose.*

"These ogres and trolls couldn't talk silently, I take it," Dammy said.

Quite right. A few barks and grunts—rather dull fellows.

"But it looks like they won," Dammy said. "Unless your boys are really our ancestors and not *erectus*. But I doubt it. You're not really Hominoidiae, I bet."

Curious idea, Sport said sadly. *Imagine people losing out to ogres and trolls! But you seem a human enough fellow, Dammy. So let's consider ourselves relatives in spite of all, even if only collaterally.* Again, Dammy shook all four hands.

How are things back home these days? Sport inquired genially. *Old dragons finally died out completely, did they? We used to see the odd one now and again—obviously only a few breeding pairs hanging on back in the hinterlands. Saw fewer every year. I remember the last one I saw.* (He graphically visualized what Dammy recognized as an iguanadon gumming foliage with toothless jaws.)

"We thought the last dinosaur cashed in his chips back in the Cretaceous," Dammy offered. "Based on the fossil record, of course."

Umm. It figures. Shy creatures. Always went off somewhere to die. We never found a dead one. Lots of stories about the Dragons' Graveyard, that sort of thing. I suppose they had a habit of heading for some sort of country that happened to be poor fossilizing ground. Knew one old fellow who claimed they swam out to sea. Trying to return to the old hatching ground, and continental drift had put an ocean between the dying dragon and his destination.

"Like lemmings," Dammy said. "Maybe so. It's as good an explanation as any. Consider the eels."

Sorry, they must be since my time—whatever it is you're referring to, that is. Eels are long skinny fish that we catch in the river. What about them?

"Both European and American eels breed in the part of the Atlantic known as the Sargasso Sea. Then they head for their home river—know instinctively which way to go. The theory is they started breeding in the Atlantic when it was just a long, skinny lake and kept on as it got wider. Sea turtles do the same sort of thing in the Pacific. Amazing, when you think of it—all those animals heading for geography that hasn't been there for a few million years."

Lots of changes, I suppose, Sport said. *But the basics we can always count on: the Endless Forest, the inexhaustible supply of game, the rivers and lakes to give us plenty of good water and all the fish we can eat—all that can't change, no matter how tribal customs vary. I suppose I'd hear nothing but barking if I went home now—but I could go off into the forest depths and forget it.*

"The tribe made it big," Dammy said. "People or ogres, or maybe a hybrid, but we spread out until we came to the end of the Endless Forest and met ourselves coming the other way."

So I suppose that Here is now a paradise indeed, Sport hazarded. *No doubt we've mastered the big-bitey-things and the big-noisy-things and the great-big-shaggy-things and so on, so that we can run down the stripey-SOB's-that-run-like-the-devil in peace.*

"Maybe it figures," Danny remarked. "Telepathy is the primitive form of communication; birds and fish and insects seem to communicate without barking, and although *H. erectus* had well-developed Broca's and Wernicke's areas, and his organized hunting suggests he could talk, his pharynx and tongue weren't capable of true verbal speech. . . ."

I'm enthralled, Sport said ecstatically. *Did we ever solve the problems of drafty caves and crap disposal? And lice and toothache and too-damn-cold and too-damn-hot? Imagine! A world where we need fear no animal . . .*

"Except man," Dammy said. "We settled down

to fighting among ourselves after we'd wiped out the hyaenodous and the cave bears and the stabbing cats. And for the best of reasons. We *had* to, to develop our character. The first hero was a man with the guts to stand up to the reigning bully, not the first man to stick a wooden spear in an enraged bull mammoth."

We have much to discuss, Sport said. *Later, back in the peace and coziness of my smooth place.*

"Like figuring out why we're hanging around here waiting to find out what old Floss or Clace or Astrobe is going to cook up next?"

Astrobe is an interesting fellow, don't you think? Sport said while digging in his ear with a hind finger, after which he courteously offered to groom Dammy, who declined.

"It's some coincidence that we both come from Earth," Dammy said.

Not at all, was the reply. *You were placed here at my express request.*

"How did you know about me?"

I didn't—not personally. But being rather lonely at first, sometime ago I arranged, if any other of the people should happen along, that he be sent to me.

"How did you get here?" Dammy asked.

It was rather odd. I was gathering long-yellow-sweet food, when a big-bitey-thing appeared quite suddenly, directly in my path, a rather narrow cleft in the rock. I turned to flee and saw a strange Person; a moment later I awakened in a place-that-was-smooth, the first of many I was to see.

"Snatched just like me," Dammy commented. "And what have you been doing since?"

Eating and eliminating, mostly, plus sleeping.

From time to time the ancestral-spirits-that-can't-get-into-the-underworld come along and take me outside for a bit of fun here in the arena. Last time it was hungry dire-beast; rather a bore, actually. It's so simple to distract the poor things into eating the fellows who run the show.

"Pitted against wild animals in the arena," Dammy mused. "And you call that fun. How often does it happen?"

Quite frequently. About once each five thousand years, I should imagine.

"Just for a second there I started to worry," Dammy said lazily. "I guess I'll take a nap. How long has it been since the last time?"

Try the pavement, Sport suggested. *About five thousand years, give or take the odd decade.*

"Oh. Then I guess I can relax." Dammy stretched out on the resilient, body-temperature surface.

How I admire your aplomb, Sport commented. *I rather doubt that I would be capable of dozing off under the circumstances.*

"What circumstances?" Dammy inquired vaguely. "You told me it's no sweat. So why not grab some shut-eye?"

The circumstance, a chilly mind-voice cut in, *that you are guilty of high crimes against the state and are unlikely to receive a recommendation for clemency.*

"Wait a minute!" Dammy blurted, sitting up. "I got a right to a mouthpiece!" He got to his feet. "And anyway, you'll have to catch me first."

Reaching deep into his inner resources—an unexpectedly shallow repository after all, Dammy noted—he levitated, floating in a vertical position just clear of the arena floor for a few moments; then he rotated to a face-down, horizontal orientation and at once shot upward so rapidly that the arena below seemed to dwindle in an instant to postage-stamp size before Dammy lost it in the intricacy of the vast city spreading below him. Far away hazy gray-green hills formed the horizon. Without conscious effort, he darted this way and that, delighted with the sensation of flying high. He was aware of a distant buzzing and then saw a swarm of gnats in the distance, a swarm which churned aimlessly for a moment before resolving itself into a stream aimed more or less in his direction. As the leading gnat grew closer, Dammy realized with surprise that it was very large for an insect—in fact that it was about the size of an F-115, and similarly ferocious in appearance. Its shock wave *boom!*ed and then it was past, only a shower of stinging pellets impinging on Dammy's exposed awareness indicating its hostile intention. Dammy easily shunted aside the projectiles, hundred-millimeter high-explosive antiaircraft cannon shells, he noted in passing. They exploded harmlessly immediately after ricocheting from his hastily erected defensive aura. The second and then three craft abreast fired equally futile bursts at him. A heavier weapon-system now approached, angled up to shoot above him, dropping a small nuclear bomb which arched sharply toward him.

Wait a minute! Dammy thought frantically. *I can't handle the heavy stuff! No fair! Help!*

"I dislike to intrude," Sport's soft audible voice spoke up. "But may I be of assistance?"

Confusedly Dammy twisted to catch a glimpse of his pal's shaggy, long-limbed form in a reclining pose, floating as easily as he himself, it seemed. "Welcome to our group," Dammy said. "But it looks like our group is about to be dispersed." He *reached*, touched the armed and down-counting bomb, now only three point oh-eight meters distant and falling at a rate of three hundred meters per second, allowing him a full one-hundredth of a second in which to act. He *thrust*, feeling the last of his strength draining away, and was aware of a vast relief as the nuke went spinning off to disappear as suddenly as the attack squadron that had launched it.

"Let's get out of here," Dammy suggested, suddenly vividly aware of his exposed position hanging unsupported, in full view, twenty-four hundred and six meters three centimeters above the capital city.

Sport was sitting across the table from him, his usually merry expression somewhat glum in the yellow glow of the guttering candle. He refilled their smeared jelly glasses from a nearly empty handblown bottle. Dammy grabbed his and took it at a gulp. It was reject grade mimblefruit brandy from Osvo 3, cut fifty-fifty with straight wood alcohol, he noticed, uncaring.

"Sport!" he exclaimed. "How? What? . . . and all the other interrogatives too," he choked, then continued silently.

I had the damnedest dream. I was flying, and things got kind of hairy, and you were with me—and here we are.

So we are, Sport agreed silently. *You are an adventurous fellow, Dammy*, he commented reproachfully. *Curious that you always manage to do the unexpected. But why did you send me that* urgent message to meet you here, in this deserted subvault?

"I didn't," Dammy managed to say aloud, wondering if his vocal apparatus were permanently damaged.

But it seemed to be quite unmistakably your voice, Sport insisted. *It was just after you'd made that remark about needing something called a 'pack of butts' and went into the male eliminatorium. I waited, but you didn't return, so I started to go in myself to see if all was well. Then I got the message, with its precise directions as to how to get here.* Sport paused to shudder.

"I have perfect confidence in your wisdom, of course, Dammy, but I don't quite see how we're to get out again, having welded the lock mechanisms to discourage pursuit." Sport was speaking aloud again, Dammy noticed; possibly he felt that, after all, his hairless friend understood barking better.

"We were in the arena," Dammy said carefully, attempting to orient himself.

"Yes, I recall it well," Sport replied. "Only two hundred of your 'years' ago, yet it's as fresh as if it were yesterday."

"It hasn't been half an hour," Dammy said desperately.

Sport looked distressed. To his surprise, Dammy felt the delicate mind-touch of his friend, probing without prior permission, a thing he had never done before.

"Oh, dear," Sport said unhappily. "This is dreadful! How could they? Or—how did they? My fault entirely; I had simply assumed too much. But there it is—no help for it now, I fear. It's up to you alone, Dammy. I'd help if I could, but you understand better than I—"

"Do I?" Dammy inquired, frowning. "What's the beef, Sport? Did I do something wrong?"

"Not wrong in any moral sense, Dammy, but tactically, perhaps. Still, I suppose it was the only way to recoup the earlier blunder."

"Tell me straight out, Sport," Dammy appealed. "What's wrong?"

Sport looked at him solemnly with large, brown monkey eyes. "You died, Dammy old fellow. I'm sorry, but there it is. You're dead."

"That was careless of me," Dammy agreed. "But I never thought it would be like this: no angels, no harps, but no little fellows with tails and horns and pitchforks, either. Maybe I better quit while I'm ahead."

"Are you willing to do so, Dammy?" Sport asked urgently.

"Sure," Dammy said emphatically. "Who wants to be a corpse?"

"Try to remember," Sport suggested. "You recall that long-ago time in the arena at Trisme? Good. Hold on to that."

"Nothing to it," Dammy said. "But after that . . ."

"Never mind that," Sport advised solemnly. "I don't quite understand what's happened here, but I feel sure your profound recollection of the arena affair is significant. So cling to that. Regard the rest as a dream. Try, Dammy; perhaps you can do it. You've gone too far for outside help to reach you. Try."

Dammy tried. . . .

* * *

Oh, dear. Sport's gentle mind-voice penetrated Dammy's restless dream. *Here it is. . . . Oh, big-horny-devils, just as I'd hoped: one longs for a challenge.*

"Two will settle for bunny wabbit," Dammy commented, and blinked against the harsh sunlight. From the same dark entry from which Sport had emerged a few minutes earlier something vast and noisy thundered, snorting with effort. Sport dropped to all fours and galloped forward as if to intercept the immense creature.

The beast he was advancing to meet was no larger, Dammy estimated, than a TD-18 dozer, and about as dainty. It was massive in build, with four legs, a flaring shield of armor behind the three-horned head. Dammy felt the ground tremble under its charge. It was, he realized, an adult *Triceratops*, alive and healthy, though apparently in a bad mood. Sport altered course to cut across in front of the monster, which ignored him to continue its blind charge. Sport halted, rose to his rear limbs, waved cheerfully to Dammy, and ran two-legged after the retreating dinosaur, which had slowed to a trot. Sport came up alongside, matched pace, reached for a grip on the nearest horn, and lightly leaped astride. The ornithischian seemed not to notice. The crowd muttered.

I'll have to stir him up a bit—Sport's comment came clearly to Dammy—*or they'll shoot this poor gentle old fellow and bring in something uglier.*

Don't go to any trouble on my account, Dammy replied.

At that moment there was an anticipatory stir among the spectators, and the pole wielders came to the alert as a second *Triceratops* emerged from the chute and skidded to a dusty halt, all four feet braced.

He's just a harmless grazer, Sport reassured Dammy, who looked around, saw the hominid doing a two-handed handstand on his puzzled steed's horns.

Then Sport shifted his weight, gripping the yard-long leftmost horn with all four hands. He began to bounce up and down, causing the reptile to give its head an impatient shake. For a moment Sport's grip was loosened, and he clung by only two hands—but he had edged outward, and now, regaining his fourhanded grip, he rode just short of the needle-pointed tip of the horny spike. The great beast was now carrying its massive head slightly lower and tilted to the left, Dammy saw, but it continued its charge as ferociously as ever. At each bound, Sport's shaggy glutei brushed the ground as he dangled beneath the horn. He hitched himself higher and, swinging up above his support, resumed his rhythmic bouncing. The horn tip dipped in response, almost grazing the pavement.

Oh, neat, Dammy commented. *If it works.*

I've done it often with aurochs, Sport replied confidently. *The trick is to know when to jump.*

Dammy could hear the harsh rasping of the burdened horn as its tip raked the resilient pavement, sending up an arc of splinters of plastic and horn. Sport, releasing his arm grips, rose to his full height and jumped up and down, maintaining a precarious balance. Dammy watched, wincing in anticipation. Then the horn tip scraped hard and dug in. For an instant it was as if the *Triceratops* had dipped his great head to sniff at the pavement;

then, as Sport leaped clear, the dinosaur was, astoundingly, standing on his head, his rear legs kicking. His body hurtled up and over, pivoting on the now deeply imbedded horn, which snapped with an almost metallic *pong!* Dammy felt the impact through his feet as the thirty-ton armored beast slammed the pavement and slid. Half-stunned, it staggered to its feet and stood swaying.

I hope it's not two throws out of three, Dammy commented, relieved to see his newfound friend on his feet, apparently unruffled.

It's technique over tonnage every time, Sport said. *Q.E.D.*

Yeah, Dammy muttered. *But what if he'd happened to land on you by accident?*

I am careful to avoid that, Sport replied. *Look out!*

Dammy whirled to find *his* assignment standing head down, all horns aimed, twenty-one point four meters distant. As Dammy turned, it snorted and charged. Dammy waited until the leading horn was a foot from his chest, then grasped it and vaulted to the beast's back. It continued its charge, modifying course as number one shook its head ponderously. Attracted by the motion, number two thundered on, head down, horns aimed at its relative's massive ribs. Number one maneuvered clumsily to face the charge, lowering his head to present the full diameter of the flaring neck shield. At the last moment Dammy hopped clear, and the two behemoths collided head-to-head with a crash like a dump truck ramming a concrete underpass. That accomplished, they trotted off companionably, side by side.

Hey, look! Sport telepathed in a surprised tone.

Dammy looked up to see a small glider with broad, varicolored wings and a slim black fuselage sailing out over the arena, apparently launched from the upper bleachers.

"Looks like old Floss, etc., can fly after all," Dammy muttered aloud, as was his habit now when Sport was out of hearing range. The colorful creature altered course to pass directly over Dammy, then banked steeply and stalled in to a feather-light landing. He strolled toward Dammy as casually as if he had just alighted from a taxicab.

"Damocles," he called cheerily. "I think perhaps this farce has gone far enough. Would you like to get out of here, have a nice dinner, and get some sleep in a real bed?"

"What about Sport? Him, too?"

"Oh. But what does that matter? My plans—"

"Sport's my pal. Where I go, he goes."

"Oh, that again, eh? Very well. May I. . . ?"

Dammy felt a tentative *touch;* then the sunlight dimmed suddenly and the crowd noise changed and he was seated at a table at the Green Corpse. Sport was seated opposite him grinning a vast grin, and Floss perched rather tentatively on his right.

"Blurb steak all around?" he inquired casually.

"Rare," Dammy said.

"Enchanting," Sport commented; then Dammy withdrew telepathic awareness as Sport fell into earnest conversation with their host.

"But, Damocles, you're *not* sulking?" Floss demanded a few moments later.

"Who are you being now? Floss, the harmless beauty lover, Clace the local big shot, or Astrobe, the Galactic VIP?" Dammy asked grumpily.

"I see no need for less than perfect candor, Damocles," Floss replied. "I see there is still much to learn of your curious life-form."

"What was all that jazz with the dinosaurs?" Dammy demanded.

"A harmless illusion designed to tease out certain response syndromes from your subconscious," Floss replied airily.

"Your methods," Dammy said severely, "are crude. Like your lies. Funny, Floss, I can always tell when you're lying."

"No doubt," Floss answered coolly. "Still, there are aspects of the situation which are, by your own admission, beyond your comprehension. Kindly accept my assurance that my actions since our first encounter are not without significance. Nor do I waste time on unimportant matters."

"So what's so important about having Sport and me clown around with a couple of brainless extinct critters?" Dammy demanded.

"Perhaps later you'll come to understand my methods, Damocles. Had I subjected you to an impressive battery of tests using electronic scoring devices with winking lights and cryptic printouts, you'd have been quite satisfied. As it was, I learned more, and more simply, I'm sure. You are still a rather juvenile being, Damocles. Have patience—and accept my assurances that I am acting in your best interests, as well as in those of your planet-fellows. I intend you no evil."

"You talk as if you're running the whole show," Dammy commented. "How about the government? Doesn't it have anything to say about all this?"

"Once, Damocles, you made jokes about 'wise old Galactic Councillors' and so on. As you then suspected, there is no such body. *I* am the government. As the supreme intellect of the Galaxy, I naturally direct its affairs."

"At least you're not modest," Dammy commented. "I knew everything out here in the Big World would be different than I expected, but I didn't expect it to be like it is."

"You've expressed curiosity as to my personal interest in yourself," Floss stated. "As to that, it was noted some time ago that your odd kind had invented a number of concepts elsewhere unknown. If you truly apprehended the vastness of the Galaxy, you'd understand how interesting—and important—the discovery of a truly unique Galaxy-view is."

"You said something about eating and sleeping," Dammy said, yawning. At that moment the turnip-like waiter appeared, to serve the juicy steaks.

"Quite so," Astrobe replied. "Eat and sleep, Damocles, and afterward we'll talk again."

Thirteen

"The problem," Dammy said, "is to figure out who's doing what to whom, and with what—or vice versa."

"It's really quite simple," Floss said. "The curious thing about matters one doesn't understand is that one doesn't understand them. What one doesn't understand seems arbitrary and meaningless. Consider: if affairs here were obvious to you, who have lived in ignorance of the very existence of the Galaxy, that would indeed be strange."

"Still, logic is logic," Dammy said, "and one and one equal two no matter where you are. So I figure the song and dance I've been getting ever since I whipped Xorialle's space-boat must be for some kind of 'reason.' "

"Why did you leave the security of your provincial home world, Damocles? What did you seek? What brought you here?"

"Aside from an idea I could do something about Earth being rated as a Class Two Special world and humanity being used for cheap labor, I guess I don't really know. I was looking for something different—and better. I had a feeling—there's something marvelous that we're all missing. It's right there, but we can't see it, or usually can't—only a glimpse now and then. I guess in a way it's the feeling junkies are trying to find—but they're on the wrong track. It's a feeling you get when you've done something worth doing. I can't explain it. But I guess I was hoping for—what? A new chance for humanity?"

"Alas, Damocles, nothing is 'new,' and 'chance' plays no role in reality. We can only hope to know what *is*."

"Where does that leave us?" Dammy inquired.

"Come along, Dammy; I want to show you something," Floss said, and rose. Dammy followed. They rode a silent elevator for a length of time which to Dammy suggested a three-hundred-story skyscraper, then abruptly halted as the door slid aside.

"This," Floss said, indicating a featureless black door set in a chalk white wall, "is a small private museum which I established some time ago, purely as a diversion, you understand." As he approached, the panel slid aside to reveal an interior of rich gloom where jeweled brightwork sparkled in glass-topped cases under the glowering stuffed heads of strange beasts.

Floss waved Dammy on. "My hobby, Damocles," he said urbanely. "An amateur collection, of course, but not without significance. Permit me to draw your attention to my Jaque bronzes." He indicated a side aisle.

"Let's skip the stalling," Dammy said bluntly. "We left a couple of questions that want me to ask them waving around in the breeze."

"Am I to deduce from that baroque expression

that you entertain curiosity as to matters already touched on?" Floss looked bored.

"You've made half a dozen little 'slips,' Doc," Dammy said tiredly. "The same old technique. We used to call it the pigeon drop. I'm slow, but I catch on after awhile. You conned me into getting into that recovery module I called the Magic Pumpkin, slick as can be. I went for the con like a rube just off a load of hay. How come, Doc? Why did you want me to come here? You had me where the hair is short right back at your big-deal hideout north of the circle. Now what's supposed to happen? And while you're at it, why not shed the fake wings and the rest of the getup?"

The being Dammy had known as Astrobe, Baron Clace, and Floss made an abrupt motion and split along its median line. The fake insectile head and thorax opened to reveal the glistening gray-wet creature inside, which unlimbered jointless arms to thrust aside the empty carapace and step free. It had a sluglike body, short, broad-footed legs, a face that was apparently a mere random cluster of sense-organ receptors.

"Very well, my boy," the crisp voice of Xorialle buzzed in Concensual Eight. "You've uncovered my little masquerade. Now what do you propose to do?"

"Maybe I'll give the old sensory nodes a tweak," Dammy said casually, and did so. "Just a sentimental gesture in remembrance of the old days when you were doing the tweaking," he added, as Xorialle quivered and the twitching subsided.

"I thought I'd pulled the caper of the century when I 'took over' the station and left in your precious 'sole link with civilization.' You're quite an actor, Doc, even without the monkey suit. Hey—speaking of monkey suits—where's my new chum, Sport? He was with us at the Corpse, but somehow I kind of forget where he went. He wouldn't be another facet of your fascinating personality, would he, Doc?"

"By no means, my boy," Xorialle said stiffly. "Kindly spare me the gloating. One should be generous in the moment of triumph, for who knows when it may be transmuted into a moment of defeat?"

"That's the politest threat I ever got, Doc. OK, just spill it and we can get on to other matters, like Class Two Special classification, you wicked old liar you."

"I've simply done my job," Xorialle declared. "And it's been a severe ordeal for me watching you pierce my finest deceptions one by one. You, an untutored—until I came along—primitive, and I, a Grand Master of the Art. Most humbling."

"Well, you could use a little humbling," Dammy said, as if kindly. "You're still a pretty arrogant old devil, you know."

"What can you mean by that, Damocles? I've confessed, stripped my soul naked as it were, and still—"

"And I still don't like being conned. Try to grasp the idea, Doc: all your fears are realized; you're out of a job. The Galactic Consensus is finished."

Xorialle made a whimpering sound and turned blindly toward the lift door, which still stood open. Dammy casually tripped him and went to the nearest case to gaze down at an array of barbaric jewelry which included a massive bracelet of dull-shining gold set with rough-cut emeralds and diamonds no larger than walnuts, a bright-polished head circlet of platinum adorned with delicate tracery, and, at one end of the case, a heavy finger ring whittled from soft wood and embellished with what resembled a wad of pink bubble gum.

"Some collection," Dammy commented. "Which one do you like best?"

"I have no preference whatever," Xorialle stated. "I merely present an assemblage of what *is*."

The next case contained a gnawed bone, an ithyphallic dwarf in a stony black material, and a slim, exquisite statuette of silver.

"By the way," Dammy said. "What did you do with Sport? I hope you didn't kill him. He was my pal."

"Have no fear, Damocles. I know all about your curious attitude toward your 'pals.' Sport, or as he was called at home, Dear-Little-Flower-Who-Yells-a-Lot, is quite safe, even comfortable, curled in slumber in his familiar smooth place. You may rest assured we haven't maintained him in good health and spirits for seventeen thousand centuries merely to dispose of him on a whim."

"If you're lying about that, I'll take you apart slowly." Dammy said.

Have no fear, planet-fellow, Astrobe's familiar silent voice sounded in Dammy's cerebrum. *I am well content. All is proceeding correctly.*

"How come," Dammy said to Xorialle, "you're switching over to mindspeak all of a sudden? And why call me planet-fellow?"

Xorialle looked as startled as his unorganized facial features permitted. "Damocles," he buzzed in his favorite C-3 dialect, "I must crave your indulgence: a matter has unaccountably escaped my attention." He edged toward the open lift door.

"Stand fast," Dammy commanded. "You forgot to answer my question."

"I called you planet-fellow inadvertently," he stated. "I hadn't meant to let it slip, but in fact, I am as human as you. Of course I represent an evolutionary alternative, but my roots go back to *Ramapithecus*, only a few million years ago. My recent visit to the old home world was just out of curiosity, you understand, to see for myself how matters had proceeded since my time. I was naturally much dismayed to find my branch of the primata quite extinct, killed off by your savage forebears."

"Some speech," Dammy said indifferently. "It's too bad I know you'd rather lie than eat. Otherwise it could have been an interesting story."

"Dammy! You wrong me—as my collateral descendants were wronged by your ancestors."

"Crap," Dammy said succinctly. "Get over there, Doc, away from the door. Skip the 'poor downtrodden us' line and let me in on why you brought me up here."

"As to that—" Xorialle started.

"Skip it," Dammy said, and probed suddenly in Xorialle's current-actions memories—and met an impervious blankness, behind which energies flickered restlessly.

Never mind, Dammy, Astrobe spoke suddenly. *Let him be. The poor creature is a mere tool; he knows little of value to you. Simply carry on, and have confidence.*

Dammy advanced on the cowering Xorialle. Before he reached him, Astrobe spoke again. *Look at the exhibits, Damocles. And be kind to poor Xorialle. He's as at sea as yourself.*

"Wait a minute," Dammy said, almost snarling. "You talk as if you and Xorialle weren't the same guy."

Of course not, Dammy. Kindly cooperate. This is the hour of crisis. I appeal to you to do as I say willingly.

"Why should I?"

Because we're pals.

"Nuts! I can't be pals with a PA system that pops up between my ears every so often. Don't you have a body? What do you look like? Or maybe I don't want to know."

Fourteen

Half an hour later, after working his way up and down the aisles of the display room, Dammy confronted a roped-off area over the arched entry to which the legend HALL OF ODDITIES was lettered in the Pandex script. He stepped over the thick purple rope. Behind him, Xorialle uttered a sharp cry.

"Not there, my boy," he protested. "To your right: the HALL OF ACHIEVEMENTS."

"I'll look at both of 'em," Dammy replied. "That's why you brought me up here, isn't it? But I guess I've got to be careful not to get so smart I outsmart myself. Did you let out that yelp to con me into coming in here? Or not? Never mind, I was headed this way when you piped up, so I'll go ahead." Xorialle made anguished sounds but uttered no further protest.

In the first glass-topped case, Dammy saw stone implements—some crudely shaped pebbles, others more delicately worked core-flake tools. The final item was a carefully ground and polished disc of basalt, twenty point oh seven centimeters in diameter and two centimeters in thickness, perforated at the center by a smoothly bored hole. Dammy quickly argon-dated it at 102,000 BP.

"Aha!" Dammy said in mock admiration. "The original invention of the wheel; too bad they didn't invent a Model T Ford to put it on."

On trestles at the center of the long, crowded room was an ungainly artifact the size of a switch engine and with six-yard-high wheels, all constructed of polished brass in the delicately hand-finished style of medieval orreries and astrolabes Dammy had seen in a museum once back home.

"Looks like something Leonardo might have come up with if he'd gotten beyond the drawing stage," Dammy commented, and went on to view a bamboo-and-taut-varnished-paper airframe with a saddle on top and a heat-tarnished metal tube below.

"It's no F-115," Dammy remarked, "but it looks like it might work—with a good shaped charge of refined gunpowder. Chinese, isn't it?"

Xorialle gave no reply.

"But what would a primitive Chinese rocket plane be doing in your little private cabinet of curiosities?" Dammy queried his own query. "How old is it?" Not waiting for a reply, Dammy *felt* mentally of the dry bamboo cells, noting the C^{12}/C^{14} ratio. "Nine hundred and fifty years, give or take the age of a bottle of good brandy," he estimated.

While Xorialle sat slumped in an easy chair by a tall window through which the Pepsi-cola-colored twilight gleamed, Dammy went on to examine a case full of electric motors of various sizes, all appearing to have been hammered out of sheet iron, and all with spidery Arabic script designating their potencies in terms of camel power. The machines powered by the motors occupied the adjacent case: mostly tools for jewel working, Dammy decided, and moved on to a display of hand-drawn charts showing recognizable outlines of Florida, Cape Cod, Tierra del Fuego, and Antarctica, the last somewhat misshapen, it appeared, until Dammy noticed that it represented an ice-free continent. He found the Great Lakes drawn by a shaky hand with the adjacent legend "Heere theere bee Tygers."

"Funny kind of place," Dammy commented, "but it's got a reason. We'll work here together until I know the reason—you and the man you killed. Does it make you uncomfortable?"

"So, Damocles," Xorialle said sternly, "you've had your fun—now run for your life!"

"You staged it just for me to look at, didn't you, Doc? The burned-out wreck, the corpse—and nothing else. I suppose the squad of cops was blown right out of sight. Was I supposed to start whimpering for mercy when I saw wonderful, irreplaceable old me dead and incinerated? It's dopey. You're floundering."

It's all right, Dammy, a familiar, cheery voice said silently in his head. He turned at a sound to see Sport step from the lift, a broad smile displaying his large yellow incisors. Dammy embraced him impulsively.

"You sneaked off," he charged. "I was so busy stuffing my innards I didn't even notice. I've been sweating you out, old buddy."

"To be sure," Sport said awkwardly in Lithuanian.

"Now, Dammy, it's time to stop tormenting this poor fellow and get on with business."

"What business? I was just trying to find out what the idea was of all this horsing around."

"But, Dammy, you already have the data," Sport expostulated mildly. "Time now to pause and assess."

"Data are something I'm fresh out of," Dammy retorted.

Pause, Dammy. A silent suggestion (command?) interrupted Dammy's protest. *Consider: have you not conducted yourself in a somewhat feckless fashion during your brief stay here at Trisme? Think back to the moment of your arrival.*

"Well," Dammy muttered, "I faked the cops out of position, but before I could get clear I ran into Orf and his boys—but I conned Bloot into bringing me over here. . . ."

Dammy; at every step you've done precisely as they hoped.

"*Nuts!*" Dammy barked. "I've had these clowns off balance every minute!"

Your most serious error was in permitting yourself to be finessed into "evoking a simulacrum" of yourself. That was serious inasmuch as it forced you to divide your forces, as it were. It was necessary to impart a portion of your resources to the false persona—thus the dullness and aimlessness of your behavior in the very hour of crisis and in the attainment radius of victory.

"Whattaya mean, finessed?" Dammy demanded angrily. "That was my own idea, and a good one."

"Think back, Damocles. Remember," Sport suggested.

"Who'm I talking to, Sport, you or Astrobe?" Dammy objected.

A distinction without a difference, Astrobe said gently.

"You mean—*you're* Astrobe?" Dammy gasped out, staring incredulously at his friend's simian face.

"Quite right," Sport said in Zulese. "But let's discuss that later. At the moment more important matters are at hand. Remember the moment of your arrival. Try, Dammy. It's important that you understand completely.

Prize," Dammy thought. *Three of spades. . . .*

As the *chime!* sounded, Dammy was tense, ready . . . . He swiftly reviewed the lore in his memory and recalled that for a category 12 VS transport capsule in mode orynx (nonscheduled) all approach and docking maneuvers were handled by Nexus directly. Ergo, he had merely to wait patiently until the capsule was disconstituted in accordance with current energy conservation directives.

ATTENTION! a soundless voice struck at him like a hammer blow. *YOU, ALIEN BEING, WILL NOW TAKE THE FOLLOWING ACTION.* (Intricate instructions followed.)

But, Dammy objected, *that's awful risky business—and I'm going to need all my marbles in place to handle these superwhatevertheyares!*

COMPLY WITH INSTRUCTIONS AT ONCE! came the unyielding reply. Reluctantly, Dammy did so. At once, a wave of vertigo sent him to his knees. He barely noticed the gentle *plop!* as the imprisoning capsule dematerialized around him. He blinked in the sudden gloom to clear his vision. Half a dozen Trismans of Class Ten were formed up in a semicircle around him, fingering crude scimitars.

"Hold it, fellows," he called. "I'm here to report a kidnapping. A Vocile Napt, I think it was—that was at first, then this other character—Astrobe, he calls himself—stuck his oar in—and there was a gang of Teest running around loose out in Vang Sector. . . ."

"Wait a minute," Dammy said groggily. "That wasn't me, that was *him.*"

Precisely, Dammy, Astrobe's calm voice reassured Dammy. He stood, blinking around him at the curiously assorted displays in Xorialle's museum, at the sluglike Xorialle, and at Sport facing him expectantly.

"Wow," he commented. "Now I'm *really* mixed up. I remember doing it, and I remember standing over by the door watching him do it. How do I know what's *really* happening?"

Reality, Astrobe said, *is that which (to a normal mind) appears to be reality.*

"Cool," Dammy acknowledged. "But who was the bird that ordered me to split off a class-four simulacrum?"

"That was just old Xorialle here, linked up via encephalodyne with a few other local officials," Sport replied offhandedly. Xorialle edged toward the door.

"Funny," Dammy said. "I remember a lot of comedy about my neat pink hat, and then—hey! I also remember being tossed into the cooler by Bloot—only he was busy at the time chauffering me around town. Then—zap!—they grabbed me coming out of that dive—only I was already outside. Then—" Dammy paused to gulp. "One of me was killed by a bomb."

"Do you remember the moment of the explosion?" Sport inquired in Skånsk.

"No, thanks, not from the scene, if that's what you mean. But I heard it from just around the corner."

"Dammy, something very odd has occurred—but very fortunate. In the instant of the explosion, your ego-gestalt transferred to its alternate nervous system, it appears." Sport was now speaking Etruscan.

"That's what Xorialle said," Dammy commented. "Where does that leave us?"

"It's that which brought me here in haste," Sport said in Gullah. "Dammy," he went on gently, "I must ask you to attempt something which is sure to be unpleasant and may prove fatal."

"Swell. Just what I was hoping for. But first tell me a few things."

"Of course." Sport's French was that of the Latin Quarter circa 1920, Dammy noted.

"Some seventeen hundred millennia ago," Sport went on, "a Concensual survey team on a routine sweep of Vang Sector encountered the system of Sol with its eleven planets and selected the heavy double in the third orbit for sampling. As a result, I was kidnapped and transmitted to the Consensual then-capital, where a routine potential assessment turned up some anomalous data. Accordingly, I was placed in category Yunt and monitored closely for some hundred thousand years, at the end of which period I was foolishly classified Class Two Routine and released to category Bist status (with prerogatives). This of course afforded me the opportunity to learn to read and to begin to assess the exocosm."

Sport paused to sigh. Dammy turned at a sound. Xorialle scuttled across the space separating him from the lift shaft and leaped through the opening. Dammy followed and looked down the shaft. It ended ten feet below in a carpeted floor. Dammy recognized the office where Floss-Clace had interviewed him. Xorialle was at the closet door taking out a hangar on which was draped a costume that Dammy recognized as that which the alien had been wearing at their first meeting. He donned it quickly and, looking up, waved a hand at Dammy.

"Good-bye, my boy," he said. "Perhaps we'll meet again some day." He exited quickly.

"It's as well," Sport said. "After all, he wasn't by any means all bad."

"OK, we were to where you were assessing the exocosm."

"Quite. It wasn't for some million years thereafter that Concensual authorities began to sense that somewhere they had made an error, and still longer before they realized that it was I, the primitive zoo-dweller, at the root of the problem—I, noting certain inequities and absurdities in Concensual society, had quite ingenuously begun to take the obviously required actions, influencing affairs by nonobjective meddling. By two hundred thousand years ago, the full enormity of the problem had dawned upon them."

"It hasn't dawned on me yet, Sport," Dammy commented. "How about skipping over a few geologic eras and getting to the point."

"A human being alive continuously for over one and a half millions of years will naturally mature to exploit his full potential. I am, so far, the only man to do so."

"Once old Doc Xorialle called me the ultimax man," Dammy said thoughtfully. "But he was wrong: *you're* the ultimax man."

"Poor Xorialle, a high-ranking official, thought he saw a way out. Confronted with the situation in which the great and powerful Galactic Concensus was being effectively ruled by a lone imprisoned superbeing, he thought to rear up a rival and to introduce you into the equation in opposition to me. Only slowly did the full ineptitude of his grossly illegal one-being ploy dawn on him. Because now, of course, there are two of us, and a world populated by another two billion humans, any one of whom is capable, potentially, of ordering the Galaxy."

"Wow," Dammy commented softly. "Now back to the something painful you mentioned. . . ."

"For the first and only time since *Homo* emerged from his anthropoid forebears," Sport said, "a human intellect has been afforded the opportunity to live on beyond the normal 1000-year span to full maturity. This is not a matter of education, only of fulfillment, like a butterfly maturing in the chrysalis. Ontogeny recapitulates phylogeny: from conception to age three, a human fetus encompasses seven hundred million years of organic evolution—from single cell to speech in forty-five months. Thereafter, he begins to explore the vast potential of his human nervous system—and is cut down before the process is well begun. In my case, removed from environmental dangers at age three and carefully fed and tended, I proceeded at the same fantastic rate for one point-seven million years, to completion. Xorialle, by forcing you to extend yourself, was able to elicit a major part of the same developmental potential. However, Dammy, an important segment of your ego gestalt was of necessity split off to vitalize the simulacrum you were so unfortunately pressured into evoking. Thus you, as you stand before me, are incomplete, lacking your full powers."

"Nuts," Dammy said flatly. "I can still—" He broke off, concentrating. "I see what you mean," he concluded. "I'm not quite back where I started, but for an ordinary Joe, I'm in way over my head."

"There may be a way out, Dammy. Your alter ego is not quite dead, merely withdrawn into a vital survival state. You may be able . . ."

Pressure crushed him as thin as the plane of fracture of a diamond and as broad as the Galaxy. He got a finger under one edge and started it rolling up. Then he hammered the ends, compressing it into a disc which he crumpled into a hard sphere half an inch in diameter. The pain was a sensation that transcended mere agony. He gathered his forces and struck back at it—a blow at emptiness. The sphere expanded, ballooned to encompass the distant radio galaxies.

Maybe that was the Big Bang, he said, or thought, in immense cast-iron words. He focused his intellect, found the Center of All Things, and looked down at horror. He tried a step; it worked. Ignoring the crunch and crumble of incinerated tissue, he walked. It was across the Galaxy, he knew. But he had to try. The stink bothered him. He plucked at charred rags dangling from exposed bones and went on. . . .

* * *

"Dammy!" Sport's tone was pleading. Dammy opened his eyes and looked up at his friend's face looming over him like a grotesque moon. "Don't try any more, Dammy. Rest now. For an instant—but no, you're alive. Rest now."

"Yeah, but," Dammy managed. Behind Sport, the elevator door *whoosh!*ed open. A blackened scarecrow stood there. It wavered on its feet, then advanced, thrust out crumbled black hands.

"Made it," the monstrous thing croaked as it fell.

Dammy felt the impact of the floor even as he heard the thud of the falling corpse two meters away. For a moment his thoughts were a maelstrom of fragmentary impressions; then he steadied himself and reached out to touch the writhing, sunlike surface of that which was the mind of Sport.

"Yes, we made it, Sport," he said. "We managed to merge. I'm *me* again."

Ten minutes later, Dammy completed his second tour of the HALL OF ODDITIES.

"The first time I didn't get it," he acknowledged. "Now I do. For all these centuries, every time a man got it together enough to make a major new discovery or invention, old Xorialle was there to nip it in the bud."

"Not quite every time, Dammy," Sport pointed out. "You made it in spite of the mutilation of the species by the meddling of the Concensus. Once the biological evolution was complete, in my time, the rest was inevitable. When Xorialle tried his desperate gambit, it was already too late. Humanity has already passed the crisis. Now there is only the future."

"Sure," Dammy said as if indifferently, as his thoughts leaped ahead to the prospect of two billion humans, educated, *aware*, ready to receive their inheritance of space-time.

"Come on, Sport," he said. "Let's go home."